Hidden Moon

Hot Moon Rising Book 4

By
Afton Locke

Copyright © 2016 by Afton Locke
ISBN: 978-1-68361-022-9
Cover art by Mina Carter

Published by Decadent Publishing Company, LLC
Look for us online at:
www.decadentpublishing.com

~A Note from the Author~

Dear Reader:

When Desiree Holt invited me to be part of her Hot Moon Rising series, I was honored and excited. I've been to Florida several times, and Moonlight is the perfect setting for a wolf pack. Learning about her admiration of wolves has helped me understand them and love them more, too. Writing in a shared world is challenging and exciting, and it's fun to belong to a "pack" of authors.

Like Alan, the hero in my story, I don't always fit into the everyday world. I know how difficult and painful that can be, especially when one has escaped the problem for a while, only to be dragged back into it when least expected. Love heals all differences—economic, racial, political, health-related, or even a wolf-shifter mutation.

I love hearing from readers, so please contact me at: aftonlocke@aol.com

Afton Locke

Dedication

This story is dedicated to Tupac. As a paranormal writer, I'm increasingly fascinated by the spiritual realm and how it enhances creativity. Watching a documentary about his life filled me with inspiration for the hero of the story. While riding to Thanksgiving dinner, I struggled to find the rocket fuel to launch this story off the ground. When he told me the essence of my book was one word—*blood*—violence vs. pack kinship—everything fell into place and I couldn't wait to start writing.

Moonlight Wolf Pack

Charlie Aquino (human) - Detective for the sheriff's gang task force for Palmetto County Sheriff's Department. His partner is Jesse Farrell.
- Mate: Liana Cosa

Liana Cosa Aquino – Refugee from a different pack. She works part-time as a waitress at Moonlight Diner.
- Mate: Charlie Aquino

Alexa Martin Farrell – Left her pack over a disagreement with her alpha. She moved to Florida and helped the pack find a small community of cottages in Moonlight, Florida. She works as an Internet researcher and gets jobs through her online website. She also does research for The Defenders.
- Mate: Jesse Farrell

Jesse Farrell (human) – Detective for the sheriff's gang task force for Palmetto County Sheriff's Department. His partner is Charlie Aquino.
- Mate: Alexa Martin (who saved him when on assignment he was attacked by a gang)

Riesa Marlowe (human) – A psychic who helped locate Hannah Raines.
- Mate: Derek Sawyer

Hannah Raines Molina – She was kidnapped and saved by Jesse and Charlie with the help of Riesa Marlowe, a psychic. Works as Alexa Martin's research assistant.
- Mate: Rand Molina

Rand Molina - Derek's second-in-command in the Moonlight pack. Partners with Derek Sawyer at The Defenders, a private security agency.
- Mate: Hannah Raines

Derek Sawyer – Alpha of a small pack, most of their original clan was destroyed when developers took the land they were living on and many of their pack were killed by hunters. They hid in an abandoned orange grove until Alexa offered them the bungalows in exchange for their help. He and the others have embraced Jesse & Alexa and Charlie & Liana and given the female shifters a new sense of belonging.
- Partners with Rand Molina at The Defenders Agency, a private security and bodyguard agency.
- Mate: Riesa Marlowe

The Defenders Agency - A private security and bodyguard agency formed by Rand and Derek once they were established in the little enclave of cottages. It provides good income for the pack. A majority of the pack is involved in the cases they take.
Jesse and Charlie are their contacts with the sheriff's department and also refer many cases to them.

Chapter One

Reston, VA

"I see you skipped lunch again. Would you like an orange?"

Alan Shifflett looked up from his computer monitor and the zillion lines of code he'd wrestled with all day. His fingers, stiff and cold on the keyboard, needed a break. These damn northern winters never seemed to end.

His co-worker looked easier on the eyes than logic statements, but her long, dark hair and form-fitting blouse—unbuttoned a little too low—did nothing to warm him up.

"No thanks, Pam. I hate oranges."

The expectant glow in her eyes snuffed out like a candle. How long would it take her to realize he didn't date? Not even blondes like.... No, he wouldn't go there. Shelley was a schoolboy fantasy. A dream-turned-nightmare.

Seeing couples in the street got to him sometimes, reminding him what he missed out on. On nights of the half-moon, he wrestled the sheets, desperate to shove his aching cock into a hot body. Hers. He dreamed of closing his teeth around a soft neck in the mating bond. Marking his stamp on a woman. Making her his.

Luckily, those moons only happened once a month.

Most of his co-workers suspected he was gay, but he didn't care. At least they were smart enough to leave him alone. He came here to get a paycheck, not hang out at the water cooler and eat sickening-sweet donuts.

In his high-rise apartment down the street, a huge porterhouse steak waited for him in the fridge. He looked forward to cooking it medium-rare and gulping it down with a glass of Merlot. He had a simple life, all right, but most of the people here, hunched over their keyboards in their cubes, thrived on the same thing.

How do they stand it? he'd wondered when he'd first arrived five years ago from Homeland. The small town in southern Georgia—spitting distance from the Okefenokee Swamp—was the complete opposite of this place. Suppressing the urge to shift had driven him crazy, but working out at the gym, freezing his ass off, and being away from his old pack had washed the urge right out of him. As long as he stayed alone in his apartment on nights of the half-moon, nothing happened.

Luckily, he resembled a regular guy in human form. To blend into the corporate world better, he'd shaved off his shaggy, rust-brown hair and tamed his beard into a neat goatee. Because he didn't shift anymore, the scabby patches on his face from his sharp teeth had cleared up.

No one would ever suspect he was a shifter with an inherited mutation that made him ugly and violent. If anybody saw his snaggly ass in wolf form roaming the streets, he'd probably never even make it to the pound. He'd be shot on sight.

Eventually, he'd figured out if he stayed here, away from his old pack and his homeland, he was normal. Living the life of a boring human was a small price to pay for it.

Stretching, he focused on the computer code again. Only two hours until quitting time. He lived by the clock here. It dictated when he ate and slept. No more running wild through the swamp with sandy dirt under his paws. Not in this place. His car sat in a parking garage, and he had to take an elevator down seven floors to get to it.

When a new email arrived, he hoped the testers hadn't found another software bug. The subject line, *Your Father*, gripped his heart with an icy fist. He didn't recognize the email address of the sender, but he didn't exactly keep in touch with the pack. Or his father, either, for that matter.

The ornery cuss called him a coward, and good riddance, for leaving. A month later, he'd called Alan once, in the wee hours of the morning.

"Dad? Do you know what time it is?"

"I did not call to find out what time it is. I called to talk some sense into you and get you back home where you belong. But it's probably no use."

Then he'd hung up.

The email message came from Shelley Fields, the only woman he'd ever seen as a potential mate. That alone sent the blood draining from his head. *She must not have married, either.*

Alan, a lot has happened since you left the pack. About three years ago, we were attacked by a rival pack led by a vicious alpha. Many were killed, but

*some of us fled from Georgia to Central Florida to
live off the land. Six months ago, we finally moved
into homes and named our little town Moonlight.*

*Your father fixed up an abandoned building and
turned it into a restaurant like the one he ran in
Georgia. Last month, he found out he's suffering
from heart failure and is now too weak to run
Moonlight Diner. Please come as soon as you can.*

The rest of the email provided addresses and
travel directions. *Oh my God.* So much had happened
since he'd been away, and he hadn't had a clue. The
words *heart failure*, though, really made him swoon
in his seat. Dad was an old wolf, nearing the end of
his lifespan.

He had to go to Moonlight, straighten things out,
and see Dad before...the end. After exhaling a shaky
sigh, he dug his fingers into his scalp. Vacation time
wasn't an issue. He'd never taken one, so he had
plenty of hours saved up.

His breath caught in his throat, competing with a
wave of nausea. A cold sweat broke out across his
shoulder blades, dampening his business shirt.

No. I can't go back to them. I can't!

Even though the pack lived somewhere new,
Florida was still the south. Being around those wolves
again would stir him up, regardless. He glanced at the
calendar. *Shit!* The half-moon was tomorrow. How
could he revert to being a freak when he thought he'd
finally escaped that misery for good? The normal life
he'd built so carefully over the last five years crashed
around his head, harder than a tidal wave.

Before he could stop himself, he pounded his fist
on the desk. Cold coffee jumped in his cup, and
nearby conversations halted. He hadn't meant to hit

it so hard. The mere idea of confronting his old pack again must have released the beast in him an inch or two. If he didn't get himself under control, he'd blow his cover, his job, and his life here.

Pacing inside the confining area of his cube, he took several deep breaths until his hammering heartbeat calmed down. He hoped to hell he could control the beast when he arrived in Florida, or they'd be sorry they summoned him.

***

Moonlight, FL

Shelley Fields rushed from Moonlight Diner's kitchen, balancing a heavy tray on her shoulder. After setting down replacement fried chicken platters in front of a family of four—because they complained to the waitress the originals were too greasy—she muttered the meal would be on the house and trotted toward the kitchen again.

Curtis King gripped her elbow. "Hey, slow down before you drop."

The warmth in his blue eyes eased her pace a notch or two. His face, lean and wolfish even in human form, felt as familiar to her as her most comfortable pair of shoes.

"I wish I could." She brushed back a hank of hair that had slid out of its rubber band. "But I've got hungry tourists to satisfy."

From what she could tell so far, Winter seemed to be the diner's busiest season. Don Shifflett picked a fine time to have heart problems. She caught the rubber band as it fell on her shoulder. In high school, she'd practically worshipped her curling iron, not setting foot in public until every hair lay perfectly. Now, she worked so hard she never gave her hair a second thought unless it got in her way.

"I swept and emptied the trash," Curtis said. "What else can I do to help?"

"Nothing."

The scar peeping out from his dark fringe of bangs twisted her belly with guilt. If it hadn't been for her, he never would have gotten into a near-fatal fight during senior prom. Until then, he'd been considered the best looking male in the pack. Most handsome wolf, too, with his perfect black coat and blue eyes.

"I insist," he argued, following her into the kitchen.

"But you work hard all day at your distribution business," she protested. He sold her highest quality oranges to specialty shops that made orange liqueur, marmalade, and the like.

"So do you," he argued. "As if growing most of our food isn't enough, now you're prepping it, ordering it, and God knows what else."

"My helping out is temporary." She handed him a potato peeler. "All right. Care to peel some potatoes?"

"No problem." He winked at her. "When you come up for air, we need to talk."

"Sure." She grabbed a tray of subs and salads and escaped to the dining room.

She wished she could escape their conversation as easily. He'd been hinting at marriage for a while. The distribution business he'd managed to keep alive after the attack and through the pack's rebuilding efforts used to occupy most of his time. Since he'd expanded it in the last couple of months, hiring someone to share his traveling responsibilities, the hints had grown stronger.

After a couple of hours, the dinner rush finally died down. Most of the tourists cleared out, leaving the pack members to linger until closing time. Derek Sawyer, the pack's Alpha, sipped a glass of iced tea at the breakfast counter while chatting with Rand Molina. The official pack meetings were held here, but tonight the shifters ate and socialized.

At least being busy didn't give her much chance to think, especially about the email she'd sent yesterday. She plopped into a wooden chair at a corner table where Curtis worked on a piece of key lime pie. Her feet throbbed and her back ached, but she did her best to hide her weariness from him.

"I spoke to Derek about getting you some help."

Irritation prickled her neck. "I didn't ask you to."

"Well, somebody had to." He tossed his fork onto the empty plate. "Shelley, it's about time you became my wife and mate."

"But—"

He seized her wrist so suddenly she gasped. "No more excuses. We've slept together. We've dated off and on since high school back in Georgia. Hell, we were voted prom king and queen. We're part of the pack's history. What's left of it."

"I know." *Is that tired voice mine?*

"Then why can't we seal it with the mating bond and a wedding?" His mouth curved into a grin. "I'd be satisfied with the bond, but I thought women loved weddings."

A wave of bone-draining fatigue, which had nothing to do with the long hours, washed over her. Why couldn't she say yes and be done with it? Would accepting Curtis as her mate be so bad? He knew her better than anyone, and they cared about each other. She'd known him so long she couldn't imagine him not being in her life.

But she couldn't stop picturing Alan's face. If Curtis could make her feel even half of what she did for her old classmate, she'd marry him in a heartbeat.

When he let go, she toyed with his fork, anxious to clear the table instead of answer him. *Everything happens for a reason,* Mom often said. When Don's illness brought Alan back to her, Shelley hoped she'd realize he meant nothing to her. Only then could she finally give Curtis the commitment he deserved.

"Soon," she mumbled. "I'll give you my answer soon."

"I've heard that before." Curtis grimaced and looked away. "I really ought to find another woman. You know that?"

She sensed he'd slept with human females on his business trips. Who could blame him? Working so hard often made her too exhausted for sex, and when she wasn't tired, it hardly seemed worth the bother. Nevertheless, he kept returning to her, asking for a commitment.

"I'm not blowing you off this time." She covered his hand with hers. "I'll give you my answer in a few days, I swear."

His voice dropped. "You're serious, aren't you?"

"Yes, I am." She stood. "I'm going to flip the *Closed* sign. You can help me get everybody out."

Curtis smiled, revealing perfect white teeth. "You got it."

When the front door opened, Shelley wished she'd flipped the sign earlier. She assumed the strange man walking in with halting steps was a lost tourist. A business traveler, by the looks of his khaki pants, oxford shirt, shaved head, and close-cropped beard. The blood rushing through her veins knew differently.

Alan was here.

As soon as Alan stepped into Moonlight Diner, he wished he could turn around and walk out. Getting off the plane at the Sarasota-Bradenton International Airport and sniffing the warm southern air had kicked him straight to the past. According to the directions Shelley had sent, the diner was on the way to his father's cottage, so he'd stopped here first.

Swallowing hard, he glanced at the paneled walls adorned with pictures of nearby farmland. The place looked almost the same as the diner Dad had run in Georgia. Smelled the same, too—a mixture of fried burgers and orange air freshener.

Several pack members turned to ogle him. He froze—a deer in the headlights of their steady stares—and gritted his teeth.

The sound of a breaking dish pulled him out of his trance. When he turned to see what had happened, he found a blonde woman staring at him. She held up empty, work-worn hands. Practical, shoulder-length hair had replaced her long tresses. He let his gaze drift down her white tank top—stained with food but showcasing her perfect breasts—to a pair of short denim cutoffs, long, creamy legs, and the broken plate on the floor.

Shelley. Oh God. Shelley....

Her clothes blurred before his eyes, turning into a pink satin prom dress. No sleeves. Just silky, bare shoulders, begging to be caressed. His primitive wolf brain unlocked the scent of carnations until he stood in the schoolyard again back in Georgia.

His fingers trembled as he extended the corsage.

"I-I brought this for you."

But the bad feeling in his gut intensified when he realized she already wore one. A bigger, classier arrangement than the scraggly mass of blooms he'd assembled. When the couples standing around them snickered, her hazel eyes changed from soft but guarded to hard and mocking.

"What on earth would I do with that sorry thing?" she asked as she tossed it to the ground.

"Guys usually give them to their dates." He swallowed, willing his body not to shake. "I am your date, aren't I? You asked me to meet you here."

"You?" She raised her chin. "Be serious. What would I want with you?"

He'd been set up. The invitation he'd received in his locker smelled like her perfume and was written in her handwriting. One of her friends must have forged it. Hell, the whole school was probably in on it. And here he stood, the biggest fool of all time.

The snickers bubbled into full-blown laughter. Each hacked into him with the force of a machete, pushing a primitive, dangerous button deep in his brain.

When Curtis stepped to her side, she wrapped her arm around him. "I already have a date."

"I see." He cleared the roughness in his throat. "I must have made a mistake."

"Or gotten carried away by a wet dream." Curtis sneered. "Beat it, Scabs. You couldn't get a date if you paid a million dollars for it. Even an old hooker would throw up at the sight of you."

Alan's shaking intensified until he dropped to all fours. Before he could stop it, the most violent shift of his life racked him from limb to limb. When the transformation was complete, his classmates laughed even harder.

But when he lunged forward with snapping jaws, the humor died. The taste of Curtis's shredded tuxedo, mixed with his blood, was as clear today as the scent of carnations. Homeland High's senior prom…. A night he would never forget.

Alan shook himself, dragging his mind back to the present. He blinked, finally noticing the man standing next to Shelley. Curtis King. The man jerked as if he'd remembered the attack as clearly.

"Well, if it isn't Scabs," he drawled.

Some male laughs volleyed from the breakfast counter across the room. The urge to shift ripped through Alan's gut and radiated to his fingers and toes, lighting up every nerve on the way. Because of his genetic mutation, he wasn't the typical majestic wolf people admired. He had scabby, hairless spots in his fur, snaggly teeth, and a violent temper.

He was the freak of the wolf world.

He forced himself to think of flow charts and If/Then logic, one orderly branch leading to another. It didn't work.

Don't shift. Don't shift. Don't shift.

They'd laugh even harder if he gave in to the urge, and he'd end up ripping somebody's head off. What the hell? It was as if the past five years had never happened. He'd deluded himself, hoping he'd magically recovered—at least a little. Standing here among his old classmates made it clear he hadn't changed a bit.

If anything, he felt meaner than ever.

The last thing he wanted was another vicious fight with Curtis, especially with Shelley watching. Instead, he loped toward the kitchen and flung open the swinging door, harder than he intended.

"Dad?" he barked out. "Where are you?"

"He's home," Shelley said, stepping behind him. "I called not too long ago, and Rita Gomez, his caregiver, said he's fast asleep."

Caregiver? Is he really that sick?

"Are you hungry?" she asked. "We have some key lime pie left and plenty of meat loaf."

Normally, traveling would make him starved, but the emotions still swirling through him stole his appetite. Why were her earthy eyes so soft? She looked as if she wanted him for dessert.

He wasn't a stupid kid anymore. She'd looked at him that way in English class, too. A real actress. He'd actually believed she had a thing for him and was destined to be his mate. Why else would he have dressed up and showed up at the prom?

She probably played another joke on him. Maybe she'd lied about his father being sick to get him down here. From what he could tell, Moonlight was a small town. Had the pack gotten so bored it looked for more entertainment at his expense?

"No, thanks. I'll head over there now using the directions you gave me. I could use some sleep myself."

"Don't be in such a rush," Brett, one of the asshole jocks from high school days, said from across the room. "As soon as your old man passes, you'll need to know how to run this place."

"That's a scary thought," Barbara added. Had the short redhead remained Shelley's best friend? "If his scabs don't fall in the food, he'll probably attack the tourists."

"Maybe he'll boil them in a pot and serve them to us as a lunch special," Brett said.

The resulting laughter sounded as cruel as it had

on prom night, and it still had the same effect, flaying into him like a bunch of knives. Barely surviving a brutal attack hadn't blunted their bullying skills one bit. Unbelievable.

"What if he boils us?" Curtis speculated. "You know what he did to me in high school."

"Enough!" Shelley put her hands on her hips and glared around the room. "The diner is closed. Get your butts out of here. I'm tired."

Alan was already out the door, struggling to fight off a shift as a blanket of heavy, humid air hit him. Overhead, a perfect half-moon mocked him from a silvery-blue sky. Without thinking, he picked up the outdoor cigarette butt container—a heavy thing made of concrete—ready to toss it through the nearest car windshield.

"Alan!"

Shelley's voice stopped him. He dropped the container, narrowly missing his foot, and fled. When she followed, he turned his head and growled at her.

"Stay the hell away from me!"

The sooner he saw his father the faster he could be on a flight back to Dulles. He never should have come here. He'd pay for the best care available if Dad needed it, but he sure as hell wasn't going to hang around this rat-hole town and a pack who hated him as much as he hated them.

He dropped to all fours and kept running. His business casual outfit flew off him in tatters. When sharp, crooked teeth popped out, he licked the blood from his lips. The breeze tickled the bare patches through his fur, making him shiver.

"Alan, wait!"

The beast in him longed for her to shift, too, so he could roll her under him and make her submit. Growl against her soft throat and brand her with his love bite. As if that would ever happen.

Palmettos and thorny bushes ripped into him as he ran, drawing more blood. He hated the town, the pack, and himself for being such a freak. Mostly, he hated her for making him feel like a high-school failure all over again.

Chapter Two

Shelley hurtled through the thickets, batting branches away from her face as she chased Alan. Someone needed to. He was so out of control, he might hurt himself. Judging by the difficulty of his shift, she suspected he hadn't done it in a while. She pocketed the car key he'd dropped along the way.

The urge to shift overwhelmed her, too, pulling at her limbs. Her earlier fatigue melted away. She hadn't felt so alive since high school.

She stumbled over an exposed oak root and scraped her knee. It didn't stop her long. She had to catch her mate. Comfort him. Fix the horrible mistake she'd made in their past.

After realizing the woods had grown silent, she stopped. No sign of his reddish-brown fur anywhere. Where had he gone? *Don't lose him again.* She should have included instructions in her email to meet at his father's house instead of the diner. Believing her classmates had matured over the years had been a big mistake on her part. A sick parent was enough stress for him to deal with.

Barbara's condescending attitude hit her the hardest. They'd stayed best friends after graduation, but tonight made it clear she hadn't outgrown their old clique mentality.

The sound of a moan pricked her ears. In seconds, she found him and knelt by his side. He was in human form again, naked as a jaybird, and covered with scratches. His bottom lip and the area below bled where his fangs must have punctured it. Since wolves were fast healers, the wounds turned to scabs before her eyes.

Scabs. The teasing voices replayed in her head, making her cringe. No wonder he'd moved away. Curtis had been the loudest among them. While she didn't expect him to welcome Alan with open arms after their brutal fight on prom night, he could have acted more mature. Weren't they all adults now?

She brushed her fingers across his forehead. "Are you all right?"

Unable to resist, she explored the trimmed beard, too. He definitely wasn't a scruffy kid anymore, and the latest version of him looked even sexier than the one she'd fallen in love with years ago.

"I'll live." He rose to a sitting position. "And I told you to leave me alone."

"You're tired and stressed," she argued. "I'm not going anywhere until you're dressed, fed, and settled at your father's cottage."

"Yes, ma'am." The note of teasing in his quiet voice shot a thrill through her body, out to her fingertips.

He accepted her hand to help him stand. With his other, he covered a burgeoning erection. A flush of heat crested inside her like a tidal wave. Although still a slender man, his arms were heavier and more defined. So was his abdomen. Mercy. Her fingers ached to explore each plane of his body.

"You must exercise a lot," she blurted out. "I mean, not that I was looking."

"Thanks." He grinned and turned his head. "Working out at the gym helps keep my anger level low."

"I have some clothes in my truck," she told him. "Your business outfit didn't fit in around here, anyway."

She took a few steps toward the diner's parking lot but stopped when he didn't follow.

"I'd rather wear a tarp than Curtis's clothes."

So he knew they were still a couple.

"They're not his. I have a whole bag full of clothing donations for the homeless shelter in Palmetto. I would've dropped it off sooner, but I've been canning vegetables and filling in at the diner since your dad's been sick."

Still covering his privates, he followed her. "Sounds as though you're a pretty busy lady."

She shrugged. "I like to help out wherever I can."

"You've changed." His smile looked so sexy in the moonlight. The ends of his top teeth were angled instead of straight across. The little imperfection hinted at the wolf in him and gave him a boyish grin that stole her heart.

"Thank God for that," she replied. "I couldn't exactly make a career out of being a shallow beauty queen."

"But you could have been a model. You look tired."

They stopped under a large oak tree. The moonlight filtering through the branches seemed to cast a spell over them. She'd forgotten how magnetic his eyes were. Fringed by black lashes, the pools of dark chocolate looked through her and melted her heart at the same time.

His unique scent, borne on the humid night air, wrapped around her and transported her back to high school English class. In it, she smelled his traveling fatigue, anger from the diner, raw arousal, and affinity. He was her mate. She'd suspected it in school, and now the older, wiser woman—and the wolf—in her knew it as fact.

Unfortunately, the knowledge remained as inconvenient now as then. Alan hated the pack and it hated him. Since the attack, the recovering Moonlight pack had interwoven so deeply into her life, it would be impossible to separate the two. Curtis was as well. Barbara, a handy seamstress, would probably sew her wedding dress. She wouldn't be too thrilled if Shelley told her she wanted Alan instead. It might even end their friendship.

The breath halted in her lungs, too frozen to move in or out. Her gaze fastened onto his full lips. She'd dreamed of kissing him since high school. How would their lives have changed if she'd had the guts to do it back then? What if she did it now?

His sexy mouth parted. Hers did, too, so close she inhaled his warm, quick breaths. A shiver of desire rippled through her, hardening her nipples.

He pointed, breaking the spell. "I see a light. We're not far from the parking lot."

Thank goodness he'd broken it. She belonged to another man, almost. As he walked, he still covered his crotch with his hand. His erection had grown so large he could no longer conceal all of it. Shelley swallowed, trying to ignore the hot cream making her panties slide between her thighs as she walked.

Although his attraction to her appeared obvious, he'd made it clear he wanted to be left alone. Her eyes stung because she'd probably never have the only man she'd ever really wanted.

She had to tell him the truth about the prom, for the sake of her conscience if nothing else. It didn't matter whether he forgave her or not. After that, she'd figure out how to tell Curtis she'd finally made up her mind about his proposal.

She couldn't marry him. It wouldn't be fair to him when she felt such a strong attraction to someone else.

***

Inside the cab of Shelley's bronze pickup truck, Alan put on a T-shirt and a pair of worn jeans from her donation bag. They fit tight because they were too small. Not that it mattered. She'd already witnessed his bare erection in the woods. God, he hadn't been that hard since he'd dreamed about her in high school.

The bed of the truck was full of rakes, shovels, and fruit and vegetable bins.

"You've got enough tools back there to supply food for the whole pack," he commented.

"I pretty much do," she replied. "I bought a farm with money I inherited from my daddy after he died in the attack. My mom and I do most of the work."

Luckily, the other cars were already gone, giving them some privacy. He wiped his knuckles across his mouth, grimacing at the sore scabs. He was Scabs again, all right. Here he sat in Moonlight, Florida, feeling like the biggest failure who ever lived. His life in northern Virginia might have been dull, but at least he'd felt worthwhile. Like a man. No different than the others around him.

Despite his snaggly mouth, she'd looked ready to

kiss him out there in the woods. The moon must have played tricks on him. She'd never wanted him. He'd hoped she would've grown up over the years, but the rest of the pack sure hadn't. They'd acted like a bunch of schoolyard bullies in the diner, and he'd let them push his buttons again. Maybe he hadn't grown up, either.

Did she need reassurance she remained sexy by getting every man she came across to drool at her feet? She merely had to look in a mirror. Whatever game she played with him now, he didn't want any part of it.

He tipped his head and inhaled the air. Ever since their almost kiss, he'd gotten drunk off her unique scent—one he'd remembered over the years. It reminded him of a sweet, juicy orange. Inside the truck, it smelled stronger than it had been in the woods. The arousal in it, rich as a slab of key lime pie, stood out as obvious as his erection.

Knowing he made her hot helped make up for his crappy reception in the diner, but he had to focus on Dad. Miss Prom Queen wasn't going to make a fool out of him a second time.

"How is Dad?" he asked. "Tell me everything."

"He's weakened since the attack," she said.

"Why didn't you tell me sooner?" he demanded, more sharply than he intended.

"We were so busy trying to survive and build a new pack, we didn't notice at first. It started with him cutting corners at the diner. Coming in late. Closing early. Cooking less. When we asked about his health, he got really defensive." Her lips twisted in a wry smile. "You know how he can be."

"Ornery as hell," he agreed.

"He collapsed in the middle of the breakfast shift

earlier this week. We've been helping out so we can keep the doors open. He tried to convince us it was nothing. That he was just working too hard."

Alan knotted his hands in his lap. Dad couldn't die. He had the same mutation, but he dealt with it a lot better, channeling the rage into a safe level of crabbiness. Knowing he wasn't the only person on Earth with the condition didn't make Alan feel like such a freak.

"I had a few bad feelings," she admitted, "but I ignored them because he seemed so confident. Damn it. Why didn't I trust my intuition?"

"Hey, don't blame yourself. Did you call a doctor?"

"Because Don's a wolf, Derek thought it better not to."

He frowned. "What does Derek have to do with it?"

"Didn't I tell you? He's our new Alpha. Hector died in the attack."

And how many others? Alan shivered. The group in the diner tonight had been very small.

"Anyway, it took time, but we found an expert who handles our kind."

"Dad's going to die, too, isn't he?"

She reached over and covered his hand. "You know he's two hundred years old."

He swallowed, drowning in the sensations from her special touch. "I know."

After she withdrew her hand, they sat in silence for a while. Strangely enough, it felt like the most natural thing in the world. His breaths came slow and easy, and his limbs, heavy and limp, sank into the seat. Being around her had always calmed him, especially in English class at test-taking time. It was his least favorite subject, but her mere presence made the time pass effortlessly.

He glanced over at her, wondering why she hadn't started the engine yet, but the ignition key rested on the seat between her legs. He covered his face, feeling like the world's biggest idiot again.

"I have a rental car and a suitcase full of clothes. Why did I get in your truck?" he asked.

But when he reached for the door handle, she grabbed his arm. Then she pulled his car key out of her pocket and dangled it in front of him.

"Need this?"

He grabbed it. "I can't seem to think straight around you. Hey, thanks for...everything."

She'd done a lot for him tonight, but the key and the clothes were the least of it. Most importantly, she acted as if she gave a damn about him. Made him feel part of the pack.

"Don't go yet. There's something I need to get off my chest."

His senses rose to full alert. What now? Her face looked so soft in the moonlight, and her eyes were wide and gentle, as if she'd opened a window to her soul. The brownish-green tint reminded him of growing things—Florida's vegetation and farmland.

"Are you angry at me about anything, Shelley?"

"No, I'm angry at myself."

He settled against the seat. "I'm listening."

"There's something you need to know about prom night."

He grabbed the door handle again. "No, it's ancient history. A night I'd rather forget."

She gripped his arm. "You need to hear this. I liked you back you then, Alan. I really did."

"You had a strange way of showing it." He glared out the windshield. "I really believed you sent me that invitation. Obviously, one of your friends forged it as a joke."

"I did write it," she said quickly, letting her hand drop to the seat between them. "Before I sent it, my friend Barbara found it. When she assumed it was a practical joke, I-I went along with it. If I'd told her the truth about how I felt about you, my friends would have turned on me."

He swept a hand over his scalp. "I guess dating the school freak would have ruined your social life."

"Becoming a refugee after the pack was destroyed put it into perspective for me." Her shoulders rose. "I'm so sorry, Alan."

"You should have become an actress. Sure had me fooled."

"I never dreamed my thoughtless actions could turn into such a tragedy." She dropped her head into her palms. "Someone could have been killed."

His knuckles burned with the memory of Curtis's bones under them. The next day, he heard he'd broken the man's jaw and one of his ribs. Not to mention the loss of blood, some of which had stained Shelley's pink dress.

"Is that why you're still with Curtis?" he blurted. "Out of guilt?"

Her mouth dropped open, but her eyes looked more startled than outraged.

He held up a hand. "I didn't mean that."

"It's okay." She brushed back her hair, half of which had fallen out of her ponytail over the course of the evening. "I've grown up a lot since then and have higher priorities than peer pressure."

"Looks like you have a lot of them," he said, pointing to the bag of clothes on the floor and the dirty farm gloves on her dash. "I suspect you work too hard."

Did guilt from her past drive her to exhaustion today? Ever since he'd left, he assumed she'd never given him or that night a second thought.

"Will you forgive me, Alan? Please?"

He hesitated. What she'd done had practically cut his balls off. Being a freak had never been easy, but he'd dealt with it somehow. That night had turned him into an outcast, cut off from his pack forever.

She didn't have to tell him she'd changed. Every action, word, and glance she'd given him tonight proved it. Unable to speak, he leaned across the seat and captured her lips in a gentle kiss.

Her fingers drifted to his shoulders as the pupils widened in her hazel eyes, drinking him in.

"Does that mean yes?" she asked.

"What do you think?"

He gripped the soft, rounded shoulders he'd ached to stroke on prom night. Without breaking contact, he took her key, stuck it into the ignition, turned it, and flipped on the radio. A country song about lost love filled the charged air around them.

Her mouth went wild under his—opening, licking, giving him her hot little tongue as an offering. He sucked it hard, not wanting to let her go again. He looped an arm around her back, dragging her closer. The fabric of her tank top stretched so thin, the scorching heat of her skin burned through it.

He should have chosen a bigger pair of pants. His erection was ready to bust out of this pair. He and Shelley were mates, and nothing else mattered.

"I've always loved your scent," she whispered in his ear. "It's got an edge of aggression. Danger...."

He groaned when she squeezed his thigh, sliding her hand toward the hard bulge of his cock and gripping it. If she was playing another game on him, he didn't care. After a lifetime of no sex, he planned to enjoy every moment he could.

"You, Alan!" she cried. "I've always wanted you."

"Not as much as I've wanted you." He unhooked her bra and palmed her supple breasts—the stars of his high-school fantasies. Touching her hard nipples sent flutters of heat through his balls, tightening them. "I haven't had feelings for anyone else."

She paused, breathing hard. "Really?"

Why had he told her that?

With both hands, she unzipped his pants and released his straining cock. "Let me show you how much I've wanted you."

When her head lowered toward his spread legs, he threaded his fingers through her silky hair, helping her the rest of the way down. Oh, yeah. She owed him this and a whole lot more.

She flicked the tip of her tongue over the head of his penis, sending a fork of fire through him. He couldn't take it. The urge to shift tickled his bones, and that would definitely ruin the moment.

"Suck it. Hard."

He surrendered everything into the soft ring of her lips as it swept down him—the pack's rejection, worrying about his father, not trusting her. Each thing vanished inside her sweet mouth.

She took all of him, digging her fingertips into his hips. He forgave prom night and a whole lot more. Everything had happened so fast tonight, he could hardly absorb it. Before he knew it, he rose up and down in his seat, fucking Shelley's mouth with everything he had. Muttering things like, "*Oh my God,*" "*Shit!*" and "*I can't believe this.*" Must be the beast in him. He had no idea it would be so good at sex.

To his surprise, she didn't complain or try to restrain him. For one moment, time stood still as she looked up at him with his cock between her lips, begging his forgiveness again. No dream he'd had about her had ever topped this. A blinding tremor ripped through him, and he exploded inside her mouth.

The force of it knocked his head against the passenger door window. When he opened his eyes again, she swallowed and wiped her mouth—red and swollen—with trembling fingers. Damn, he hoped he hadn't bruised it. He'd love to see the expression on Curtis's face when he saw it, though.

He brushed her cheek. Feeling his seed clinging to her face sent an aftershock through his groin. As if she was already his woman. His mate.

"I didn't mean to be so rough," he muttered.

"I'm fine." She tore off some paper towels from the roll on the floor and handed him a couple. "It felt perfect."

"Tonight was...unbelievable," he said. "I'll always remember it."

The softness in her eyes dimmed. "Then...I mean, I thought. It's good between us, Alan. We're mates. Aren't we?"

Scent of her yearning filled the cab, making him want to come a hundred more times—in her hand, her mouth again, and most of all, between her bare thighs. At the least, he should slide his finger under her short cutoffs. Make the denim sticky and wet until she came, too.

She'd gone a long way toward erasing the past, but he'd never be able to forget the prom, and he sure as hell could never find a home in this pack.

"Stay with Curtis, Shelley." He zipped his pants and fished for the car key he'd stowed in his pocket. "I don't think starting anything between us would be a good idea."

Even though she seemed sincere, he'd be a fool to trust her again before getting to know her more. Besides, an unpredictable beast lived inside him. What if it hurt someone else, like her?

But as soon as he stepped out of the truck and closed the door, his knees buckled. The wolf in him howled, begging him to stay.

Chapter Three

Alan opened his eyes the next morning, blinking several times. *Where the hell am I?* Weak light from behind a nearby polyester curtain told him it was barely dawn. The crash of broken pottery jolted him to a sitting position on the lumpy, blue couch he laid on.

"Goddammit!" The familiar, crusty voice came from the kitchen.

"Dad?"

Right. He was in Florida. A lock of silky blonde hair brushed his memory. Shelley. Her truck. *Oh freaking God.* Morning wood strained his boxer shorts. Had the former beauty queen really gone down on him last night?

The sound of more cursing propelled him toward the kitchen. Shelley would have to wait. Feeling her sweet lips around his cock was probably just a hot dream, anyway. So was her confession about prom night.

"Hold on, Dad. I'm coming."

He rubbed his bottom lip, frowning at the ugly scab under his fingertips. As if she'd ever kiss that. Don, wearing a faded bathrobe, batted at the broken pieces of a coffee mug with a broom. He'd grown so thin!

Alan took the broom from him. "I'll clean it up. What were you trying to do?"

"Fix a lousy cup of coffee. What does it look like?"

Alan suppressed a grin. Ornery as ever. At least the man wasn't bedridden. He couldn't handle that.

"Give it back." Don grabbed for the broom. "I'm not helpless."

Where had Rita gone? While glancing around for signs of her, Alan spotted the note on the counter, saying she'd arrive at eight to fix breakfast. What if his father had been alone and fallen? Did he need round-the-clock care already? One of many questions Alan would have to figure out while here.

Someone had decorated the room in harvest gold—the way Mom had in the house back home. The same framed samplers about family adorned the walls. Prescription bottles and medical papers littered the counter, though.

"Why don't you make the coffee, and I'll take care of cleaning the spill?" Alan suggested, massaging his scalp before a headache could form.

He went ahead and made breakfast—toast, bacon, and scrambled eggs—himself. Exhausted already, he served the food and coffee and plopped into a brown vinyl chair at the kitchen table.

"This slop is barely fit for a dog." Don grimaced as he nibbled a soggy bacon strip. "Who taught you how to cook?"

Alan raised an eyebrow. "You did."

"So I did." Don looked away and slurped some coffee, staining his silver beard. "The point is you've been single too long. You could have called once in a while."

Here it came. The guilt trip for moving away from

the pack.

Alan swallowed a bite of toast, but it tasted like wood. "I did at first, but I kept getting an earful of this."

"You know you're a coward, don't you?"

The beast, asleep since the ridicule in the diner last night, stirred to life. He'd give anything to be in his cubicle right now, tapping his keyboard and feeling nothing but calm oblivion.

"I don't belong in the pack." Alan drained half his coffee mug and set it aside with a thump. "I almost freaking killed someone. Don't you remember?"

"I have the same condition you have, but I learned to handle it." Don toyed with his napkin, turning it over and over. Since when had his hands started shaking? "I could have taught you, too."

"And killed a few wolves in the process?" *Or hurt Shelley?* Alan ripped into a piece of bacon while the beast clawed the root of his spine. The urge to shift plucked his tensed muscles. "It's not a condition. It's a curse."

"Are you still crying over a few scabs?" Dad asked. "Our pack already has a beauty queen. A real man wouldn't care how he looks."

Okay, he'd matured. Looking like hell didn't bother him as much today as it did in high school. Under last night's moon, Shelley didn't seem to mind the sight of him. Broad daylight might be a different story. Again, he pushed her out of his mind. Dad was the reason for his visit. Not her.

"I'm more concerned about the violence," he finally answered. "It's stronger in me. I can't control it."

But he was going to have to try for the next few days. Or weeks? God, how long would he have to stay here? What kind of wreckage would he leave behind this time?

Because Dad wasn't exactly on his deathbed, the future hung in the air like a big question mark. It had been years since they'd shared a meal together. Mostly, he ate alone in his boring apartment. The beast relaxed, releasing its jaws from his spine. Nevertheless, Alan sat stiff and straight in his seat. Getting too attached wouldn't be a good idea. It would make his father's eventual passing even harder.

"You're younger than I am. It weakens with age." Don glared at him over the rim of his coffee mug. "I'd give anything to feel that kind of energy again."

"Shelley told me a little bit about your illness."

Don scooped some eggs into his mouth. "I'll get over it."

"Dad, a weak heart isn't a cold. It's not going to get any better." He gazed at his rental car out the window, wishing he could get in it and drive it back to the airport. "Have you made...plans?"

"What plans?" he asked with a deep scowl. "Picked out a burial plot, you mean?"

Alan looked away. "I meant your property, especially the diner. It's the nerve center of the pack."

"The diner? All I know is I need to get my sorry old ass over there so I can serve the breakfast crowd."

Alan's toast sat, dense as a rock, in his stomach. Dad was seriously in denial. Unfortunately, it fell on his shoulders to get him out of it. A few siblings would come in handy right about now. So would the support of the pack. Fat chance of getting that.

"Do you have a will?"

"I suppose so." He knit his thick silver brows. "Your mother made me write one before she passed.

At least I had a sound mind and body back then."

"Good. Who inherits your property?"

"You're an only child, aren't you? What the hell do you think?"

Alan didn't know whether to laugh or scream, but the will would make it easier to escape to his normal life.

"Got it, but you can't run the diner anymore, at least not singlehandedly."

The breakfast dishes jiggled as Don stood, shoved his chair into the table, and hobbled toward the bedroom.

"Where are you going?" Alan called after him.

"To put my cooking gear on."

"But Rita is coming at eight," Alan insisted.

"Screw the caregiver. Moonlight Diner is my life, and I'm going to run it until I drop dead." He flung open the bedroom door then clung to it, panting.

Alan rushed to his side. "Keep acting like a pigheaded fool and it'll happen sooner than later. You're dying."

"You think I don't know it?" the older man snapped.

"Then go to bed and stay there. You need to take it easy."

Dad grabbed his T-shirt with surprising strength and shoved him backward. "Fuck you!"

Alan's muscles contracted as the beast in him jumped to life. A canine lengthened, piercing his lip and drawing blood. Reminding himself his father's fear and loss spoke for him calmed the beast down in time. Barely.

"You win," Alan said with a measured breath. "Let me grab a quick shower. Then we'll go to the diner. I'll help you cook today."

What about tomorrow? He wasn't sure he could get through the day, let alone another. By tonight, he needed to have a plan in place for his father's final days. He should've known the old man would fight him every step of the way.

Alan trudged toward the bathroom. Maybe some hot water would give him the strength he needed to get through the challenge facing him. Whatever he had to do, he'd grit his fangs and do it. The sooner he could return to the sane life waiting for him up north the better.

***

Shelley unlocked Moonlight Diner and carried in a crate of oranges fresh from the grove in her family farm. She'd make her bigger, weekly delivery tomorrow. This morning, she needed to tackle payroll and clean the refrigerator, which Don had probably left dirty enough to fail a health inspection.

Much as she loved being surrounded by the pack, she hoped for some time alone. She hadn't gotten much sleep last night, and when she had, she'd dreamed of Alan—sinking his wild fangs into her neck in the mating bond while he pumped his hardness into her. She'd woken up drenched, especially her panties.

Before opening the large refrigerator to load it with oranges, she touched her lips. Because wolves were quick healers, the swelling had disappeared. Had she really torn into his pants like a dog in heat?

In high school, she'd dreamed of a romantic prom date with him. In it, she accepted his corsage, held his hand, and slow danced with him to a love ballad while she gazed into his chocolate-brown eyes. While

33

his alluring scent wrapped around them, she kissed him, slowly and tenderly. The promise of beautiful lovemaking hovered around them, but lust was not part of the picture.

Acting like a whore in a dirty, old pickup truck didn't come close to the dream. His scent had completely overpowered her, melting away the years and heating her stewing guilt to the burning point. Her recent fatigue from doing too much lately hadn't helped her self-control, either.

By looking at her, would Curtis guess what she'd done with another man? Was the truth in her eyes? After confessing her true feelings to Alan, she'd found several text messages from Curtis on her phone. Apparently, he'd spotted her empty truck in the diner lot last night and wondered where she was. She'd replied to ease his mind, relieved she could do it digitally.

As soon as she saw him today in person, though, she had to tell him she couldn't marry him. Anticipation twisted her stomach. She'd sensed Alan didn't want to hang out in Moonlight very long. Most likely, she'd end up alone. It would be better than being with the wrong man, though. Maybe she could convince him to stay. After all, they were mates.

The bell above the front door jingled as she stowed the last orange. She frowned. It was too early for the breakfast crowd. She hadn't had a chance to fire up the grill yet. Dusting off her hands, she headed to the dining room.

A thrill shot through her at the sight of Alan. He must have just showered because the neck of his shirt looked damp and he smelled like fresh soap. Underneath, his unique scent teased her, reminding her of their passionate kiss and the taste of his hardness.

She looked down at her tank top and frowned. Not even noon yet and it already had a couple of dirt smudges on it. She might as well not even bother to wear white.

Blinking, she noticed Don standing beside him, wearing his apron when he should be home resting instead. By the grim set of Alan's jaw, she suspected the older man had won an argument. Alan definitely had his hands full. Good. Maybe his father's stubbornness would keep him here for a while. At least long enough to convince him she was right for him.

"I didn't expect to see you, Mr. Shifflett," she said, hiding her attraction to his son with a poised smile. "Have a seat and I'll fix you some breakfast."

"Thanks, but we already ate," he grumbled, heading toward the kitchen. "Alan, cut some vegetables for omelets. I'll get the grill going."

"I tried, but he insisted on coming." Alan shot her a defeated grin and shrugged. "I'm going to help him out here today."

She stared at the swinging kitchen door. "Don't worry. He'll wear himself out and realize he needs to rest. That'll get through to him better than being told what to do."

When he took a step toward the kitchen, she grasped his forearm and steered him toward a corner instead.

"About last night," she murmured. "I'm sorry for the way I acted."

"You mean it wasn't a dream?" His face hardened. "I figured you'd regret it. Consider it forgotten."

Panic welled up in her when he turned to leave. "No, I meant every word I said. The wolf in me bypassed the romance, but we have time for that."

"I'm here for my father, not romance. I thought I made that clear."

A cold chill swept through her. "When Curtis arrives, I'm going to tell him I can't marry him."

"Well, don't base your decision on me." He swept a cool glance over her. "I have a job and a home to return to. I don't plan to stay."

She stuffed her hands in the pockets of her shorts. The gesture felt strange because she always kept her hands busy. At the moment, though, nothing mattered except getting to know the man she truly wanted. She forgot about the day's chores and even Curtis.

"So, what do you do for a living?" she asked.

"I'm a computer programmer. I design software."

"You were always the smart one."

"Working with logic gives me self-control." His stony expression softened. "Or at least the illusion of it. I taught myself the skills I needed and got my college degree online at night."

"Sounds like we have hard work in common." Did he use it as a distraction like she did? "I wrote you some letters after high-school graduation, but you never answered them."

"I figured they were a joke," he said without expression.

She withdrew her hand from her shorts pocket. "I want you to know I kept this."

He stared at the folded piece of notebook paper she handed him. The thing had been opened so many times it was as frayed and worn as an old scrap of cloth.

"What's that?"

"One of your poems, from English class." She

lowered her eyelids, feeling like a teenager all over again.

He opened it so slowly and carefully, she had a hard time imagining his past violence. Watching his gentle fingers made her ache to feel them on her body. He'd written about beauty, and she didn't have to ask who'd inspired him. His lips moved as he read it silently, and she fought the urge to kiss them again. He finally looked up, his eyes deep pools of melted candy.

"You kept my poem all these years?" he asked.

"I stored it in my bureau, but I brought it today, hoping I'd see you."

When he handed it back, she held up her palm. "You wrote it, so you should keep it."

"But I wrote it about you, and I'm afraid it doesn't change anything."

Should she stash it into one of the deep pockets on his cargo pants? What was the use? She folded and jammed the paper back into her own pocket as she scrambled for something to say. He clearly wanted to return to his other life and forget her. She might as well stay out of his way until he did. It would make it easier to get him out of her mind when he left...again.

The sound of a metal pan dropping to the floor pierced the quiet.

"I have to go help Dad," he mumbled as he rushed away. But when he looked back, the wolf in her gasped at the longing in his eyes.

Before she could calm the emotions swirling through her, the bell above the door jingled again.

"Hey, beautiful." A familiar kiss brushed her cheek.

Curtis was here already, and she hadn't even had coffee yet.

He eased into the nearest chair, graceful as always. "You're here early. Need any help?"

"No, thanks. Alan and his father are in the kitchen."

Still prickling from Alan's rejection, she glanced toward the kitchen door. Ripping up the old poem later might make her feel better, but she doubted it.

"Is he going to take over running the place?" The edge in his voice made it clear he wasn't thrilled at the idea.

"I don't know." *And don't care,* she thought, feeling like the spoiled teen she used to be.

He drummed his fingers on the tabletop. "Well, ask them to cook us some steak and eggs. I'm starved."

The urge to marry him to spite Alan zapped her harder than a bolt of electricity, but she had more maturity than that. She'd made her decision, and Alan's aloofness this morning gave her the nerve she needed.

She gripped his hand to still it. "We need to talk first."

"I don't like the sound of that." He narrowed his blue eyes. "You've made your decision about us, haven't you?"

She nodded, looking down at their joined hands. "Curtis, you're a very special man. I'm so thankful you're part of the pack and my life."

"But—"

Dropping her hand, she forced herself to look into his eyes. "I can't marry you."

"What?" He froze for a moment then blinked and tossed his head. "You were with him last night, weren't you?"

"No...yes. He's my mate."

Curtis stood, scraping his chair across the wooden floor. "Do me a favor and don't invite me to your wedding."

"I'm not marrying him, either," she said, her voice dull and dead.

"Well, I hope you'll be happy alone."

He reeled toward the front door and bumped into Derek on his way out.

"Sorry, man," he told the tall Alpha with a quick bow of his head.

"No problem." Derek entered and turned to her with a puzzled frown above his golden eyes. "What's with him? And you, for that matter. Did you two have an argument?"

Usually, she loved the connectedness of the pack. When one hurt, the others felt it. Today wasn't one of those days. At the moment, she wished she had a simple life to escape to like Alan did. She sniffed, fished a tissue out of her other pocket, and wiped her eyes. Were her tears for him or Curtis? Probably both—for very different reasons.

"Yes, Derek. I told him I'm not marrying him."

He straightened Curtis's chair and sat in it. "I think that's a wise decision."

"You do?"

"He's not your mate. The union would not strengthen the pack." He patted her arm. "Be patient. Your true mate will find his way to you eventually."

She wadded up the damp tissue. "I'm afraid he already has."

His brow lowered, and he leaned toward her, making him look every bit the protective wolf he was. "Alan?"

"Yes, but not to worry. He plans to leave as soon as he can."

"Good. I don't trust him."

But, for some reason, she did. He was part of the pack and belonged here. Although it might be easier to let him leave again, she couldn't. Aside from her selfish feelings, his father needed him. Her sixth sense, warning of some unseen danger, told her the pack needed him, too.

Whatever it took, she had to convince him to stay, even if her heart broke in the process.

Chapter Four

Alan groaned as he stared at the diner kitchen at the end of the day. It looked as if a hurricane had blown straight through it. Batter spills crusting on the counter. Vegetable peelings on the floor. Where to begin? He resigned himself to clean the grill first since it served as the heart of the kitchen.

Shelley had driven Dad home an hour ago to rest. The man had been more of a hindrance than a help, criticizing everything Alan did.

"I'm a computer programmer, not a restauranteur," he'd muttered more than once.

But Don had sassed him back each time, until he weakened and almost fell face first into the fryer basket. Alan needed some rest himself. Every muscle in his body ached with fatigue. The only good thing about exhaustion was it tamed the beast in him.

It also kept his mind off Shelley. The vulnerable expression on her face this morning had punched him in the chest. He'd hurt her. Despite what she'd done to him on prom night, he had no desire for revenge.

The lines of his stupid poem danced before his eyes all day. Her feelings for him were as real as that frayed piece of paper. He hoped she understood why they couldn't act on them. She'd been in and out of the diner today, cleaning and ordering supplies. Every time he looked at her, a knife twisted in his heart, reminding him what they could have.

He slid the spatula across the grill, the scrape of metal on metal matching his mood. Yeah, he could have everything if he was normal—great sex, love, family. In between orders for omelets and burgers, he'd kept picturing her soft white tank top and her shorter-than-sin shorts. Peeling them off, tossing them to the floor, and pulling her into bed while their children slept down the hall. Hazel eyes gazing up at him with love. The spatula dropped with a clatter.

My woman, the wolf in him screamed.

Well, he wasn't normal. Although he'd had the mutation his whole life, it had never been more unbearable.

I have to get out of Moonlight.

Okay, he'd run the place a whole day, and it sucked. It wouldn't have been so bad if he liked the customers. The tourists were okay, but he could do without the pack. They stared suspicious holes into him every time he set foot in the dining room. Luckily, Curtis hadn't been among them. The man had a score to settle with him. He could have Shelley, but if she didn't want him, that was their problem.

Besides, Alan already had a job—a much easier one that paid better—to return to. Living beast free gave him a great bonus. Dad clearly couldn't handle the diner anymore. As he scraped a river of black grease into the grease trough, the answer became clear.

Moonlight Diner needed to be sold.

How long would it take? Moonlight was a pretty

rural town, but it received a healthy flow of tourists. Time on the market would probably depend on the price. Hopefully, a pack member would grab it up. He closed his eyes and grimaced as he anticipated laying his decision on Dad. The man would curse him from one end of Florida to another.

When the kitchen door swung open, he caught his breath at the sight of Curtis. The guy had lousy timing for settling scores. Alan felt tired enough to collapse into the grease bucket.

"Rough day?" Curtis asked.

The man's casual tone didn't fool him. He reeked of aggression, and his arm muscles looked tenser than iron as he rocked on his heels. The prom fight loomed between them like a third person in the room. Alan's beast couldn't forget the coppery tang of the man's blood scent or the shape of his bones.

Maybe if he played nice, his old rival would go away and leave him alone.

"Yeah." Alan emptied the grease container into a bucket and grabbed the grill's cleaning brick. "Running a diner isn't easy. I don't know how Dad did it for so many years."

"Ready to throw in the towel already, eh?" Curtis shot him one of his killer smiles. Not a single snaggly tooth in his whole mouth. "Have you made plans for the place?"

Alan hesitated, but his decision would be common knowledge soon enough. Maybe Curtis himself would buy it. Why did an image of him and Shelley working here side by side twist his gut so hard?

"If Dad agrees, I want to sell it now." Alan scoured the grill with the brick, channeling his tension into the sweeping motions of his hands. "Spread the word to the rest of the pack."

He'd start there out of courtesy, but he'd make it public, if necessary.

Curtis's blue eyes lit up. "Will do. I gather you'll be leaving again?"

Alan nodded. "Once everything is settled here. I'll be back for the...." Salty heat flared behind his eyes because he couldn't say the word. *Funeral.* As irritating as Dad had acted today, Alan couldn't deny the rightness of being close to kin. And his mate.

"Of course," Curtis replied. So, why didn't he leave?

"Anything else on your mind?" Alan rinsed the brick. "I'm kind of busy here and tired as hell."

"Yeah, one more thing." Aggression poured off his rival in waves as he stalked closer to the grill. "While you're here, stay away from Shelley."

The beast in Alan stirred, wanting to punch the insolent expression off his face. It didn't much like being ordered around. Instead, he squeezed the cleaning brick, pretending the man's neck lay in its place. Although tempted to fling the rejected marriage proposal at him, too, he wasn't looking for a fight tonight.

"I intend to."

If Curtis felt so determined to mark his territory, why didn't he urinate in a circle around her? The image made Alan grin and forget his anger.

"Have a good night," the guy told him before he left the kitchen.

Have a good night? Maybe they'd both grown up. Being on the same side this time helped. If Alan decided to stay here and claim his mate, though, he'd definitely have a fight on his hands.

***

Shelley pulled into Moonlight Diner's parking lot the next morning. Dread and excitement filled her belly when she noticed Alan's rental car was the only other one here. At least Curtis didn't attack him after she'd rejected his proposal. Everyone had matured.

Butterflies fluttered in her stomach when she walked inside and discovered Alan really was alone. The ripe aroma of peppers filled the air as he cut them. When she set down a crate of oranges on the counter, he dropped the knife.

The clothes he wore must have been his own because they fit perfectly. The light-blue tank top hugged his chest the way she longed to. And his jeans. She couldn't even look at them without wanting to brush against his narrow hips and muscular thighs. They fit in here better than the dumb business getup he'd worn the day he'd arrived. He even had a black bandana tied around his head.

He stood so close to her his scent—hot and dangerous—weakened her knees. Why had she stayed with Curtis so long when she'd never wanted him half this much?

"More oranges?" He wrinkled his nose. "I don't understand how people here go through so many of them."

"Don't you like them?" she asked.

"Not really."

"Use these up first. They're riper. I have tomatoes and cucumbers in the truck, too."

He carried the crate into the storeroom, and she followed him to the refrigerator. When his hand accidentally brushed hers, she died inside because the touch reminded her of everything she'd never have—with him or anyone else.

45

"You look beat," she said. "Yesterday was rough, wasn't it?"

"I've never been so tired in my life." He rolled his eyes. "I hadn't realized running a restaurant was so hard."

"You did a good job. The food tasted good and the waiting times weren't too long."

"I couldn't have done it without your help," he said.

"We make a good team," she couldn't help saying. "Is Don home resting?"

Alan nodded. "I nearly had to tie him down. He didn't like my decision."

Her fingers froze around an orange. "What decision?"

"To sell the diner."

"Oh, Alan, no."

His dark gaze hardened. "I told you I can't stay."

"Why not?" she demanded. "Do you have wild parties every night up there? A million friends?"

"No. I live alone and do my job, which is all I need."

It sounded like a lonely, unhappy existence to her. "The pack needs you." *I need you.*

"Yeah, right." He tossed an orange so hard it bounced inside the fridge. "They need me like a hole in the head."

"Careful. The ripe ones bruise more easily." Like her heart. She grabbed his wrist, overwhelmed by the electric tingles shooting up her arm. "They don't know it yet, but I sense danger to the pack."

"I live alone because I like it," he said. "It also gives me some peace and dignity. Most of all, I'm less likely to accidentally kill somebody."

"How sad for you," she said in a small voice.

He stood abruptly, letting her hand fall. "I'll grab the other crates of vegetables. Are they in the back of your truck?"

A ball of fire bloomed in her abdomen. If she couldn't talk him into staying, there was only one other way, and it happened to be something she really wanted. She stood, too, and closed the refrigerator door.

"The vegetables can wait." She brushed the orange across her breasts, raising the nipples through the fabric of her pink shirt. "I can't."

"Jesus, Shelley. What are you trying to do?" His gaze rested on her chest, heavy as a hand, and his aroused scent charged the air.

"Leave if you have to." She dropped her hand, feeling silly for acting like a seductress. "I just ask one thing before you go. Make love with me."

"That would be a very bad idea." But his voice had a big crack in it.

"Just once," she amended. "I'll never be with another man."

"You should marry Curtis. You know him a lot better than you do me."

"You've got that right. I don't know you at all." She turned her back on him. "Get the damn crates."

As soon as he left, she tore a hunk of skin off the orange she held and took a messy bite of it. Tears spattered her cheeks, but the scents of citrus and salt couldn't cleanse away Alan's. Need, male and raw, hung in the air, tormenting her. If she wasn't his cup of tea, she could accept that, but they were mates. Why did he have to be so logical?

When he came back, he dropped the crates on the counter. His muscular arms glistened with sweat from carrying two at a time.

"Don't cry, Shelley." He hugged her close to his chest and looked down at her orange, which he'd crushed in the process. "Shit. I can't do anything right." After grabbing a nearby dish towel, he dabbed the fruity juice that had spilled on her shirt.

She batted his hand away. "I'll clean it later. I need to go. I'm not wanted here."

"Oh, I want you." The deep growl of his voice vibrated the air around them.

Her breath caught when he gripped her shoulders—hard—and bent to lick a drop of orange juice from her shirt. His breath and tongue, hot and damp, penetrated the thin fabric. Fire rippled through the nipple below.

She clutched the bandana on his head with sticky fingers. "Oh, Alan.... Don't stop."

By the look in his eyes, he couldn't if he wanted to. She'd seen that fiery expression on prom night, before he tried to knock Curtis's head off. It felt as if a beast lived inside him. Knowing she'd unleashed it made her clitoris throb.

His strong hands circled behind her, squeezed her butt, and lifted her to the counter behind her.

"Yes." She gasped when he yanked up her shirt and tugged down her bra cups. His mouth closed around her nipple. Then his teeth. The sudden pain arched her back. She barely caught herself from falling backward.

He ripped a section out of the orange and squeezed it, raining the sweet juice across over her belly. The warm nectar trickled over her sensitized flesh, sending her muscles into spasms.

"That's it, honey. Twitch for me because I'm going to make you come so hard."

She moaned, gripping his bandana for dear life

when he swirled his tongue across her belly and burrowed the tip into her navel. His beard swept across her sensitive skin, hard where his tongue had been soft. She squirmed her hips, begging him to lick her swollen flesh farther south.

Instead of pulling off her shorts, he worked from underneath, squeezing the orange over the area where her bare thigh met her hip. Then he eased his finger under the denim hem, tunneling into her heat. Sweet sensations gripped her, sending her into more contractions while his tongue followed the path his digit had made.

"You know, I'm starting to like oranges," he said.

When she unzipped her shorts and tugged down the waistband of her cotton panties, he chuckled and poured orange juice over her mound, too. She sucked in fast breaths while he combed her thatch of hair, his fingers glistening wet with fruit juice and her cream.

"Kiss me," she begged.

Instead, he dragged sticky fingers through her hair, but she didn't care. The messier the better. She wanted his seed in her mouth, her hair, and all over her body. He let his mouth hover over hers, teasing her. His tongue tip flicked hers, too, giving her a few drops of juice. Rearing into him, she bit into his sexy, full lips. She must have a beast inside her, too.

In response, he growled and kissed her hard, sucking the breath out of her lungs. Every vein inside her seemed to deflate, swallowed into her meant-to-be mate. He wasn't even inside her and her body perched on the edge, ready to come. Sex with Curtis didn't even approach this.

She reached down, fumbling with his fly. "Lock the door. Lock the damn door!"

He did. By the time he approached her, he had his

zipper down and his cock out. With shaking hands, she tried to pull off her shorts, but everything was too sticky to slide. He yanked them, and her panties, off with one hand and hopped onto the counter. After crouching on his knees, he pulled her legs around so he could enter her.

His cock was so heavy and hard as he leaned over her, it brushed her sticky belly. She couldn't help writhing under it, desperate to get it inside her where it belonged. He took a deep breath and the wild look in his eyes receded, leaving tenderness.

Don't change your mind now!

"You asked for this, Shelley." He brushed her cheek with a gentle finger while big, ragged breaths rocked his shoulders. "When I enter you, I won't be able to stop."

Her head thrashed from side to side while a relentless fire burned in her loins. "Give it all to me, Alan. Even the mating bite."

His face grew serious. "Not that. Not this time."

She threaded her fingers through the tails of his bandana, bringing his head to her breast. The skin on his face burned hotter than fire. While he sucked the orange juice lingering on her nipples, she hoped her body could satisfy everything he'd ever starved for...acceptance, peace...even love.

While the suction of his eager mouth engorged the tips of her breasts, he eased the head of his cock into her drenched slit. A small scream escaped her as her pelvic muscles embraced it. Grunting, he pushed her thighs apart farther while entering her the rest of the way.

"Alan," she muttered, out of her mind with pleasure. Every nerve ending in her core screamed, *Yes, yes, he's the one. Your mate.*

"Ready for the ride of your life?" he whispered in her ear.

"God, yes." She slid her arms around his lean waist, prepared to hold on no matter what.

He pulled out slowly and lunged back into her, so fast it stole her breath. By the second stroke, he'd become a pile-driving machine. Every powerful inch of him scraped her raw yet caressed her like silk at the same time. It felt so perfect she barely noticed the pain from her bottom slapping the wooden counter. Any harder and the cans on the nearby shelves would crash to the floor.

She grabbed his bandana again. Eventually, it slipped off his head under her frantic grip. He lifted her hips while he crouched on the counter, driving into her deeper and harder than ever. The beast in him pounded through every frustration they'd ever had, starting with prom night.

In this wild, wonderful moment, they had a future. He was part of the pack and her. *Bond us*, the wolf in her howled, but when she lifted her hair and arched her neck before him, he didn't bite. Instead, she gasped when he took her to the top. His thumb nestled against her clit, strumming the super-sensitive flesh.

Their climaxes hit so close together, she wasn't sure whose came first. They grappled each other across the counter, banging elbows and knees while her pelvis exploded with fireworks. Steel-hard contractions in her belly squeezed his cock, choking off her air and damming up her blood in its tracks.

She finally breathed again when his hot seed coated her walls. *Give me your love, Alan. Your soul. Your children....* When it was over, his heavy body covered the length of hers, pressing her into the wood beneath her. His breaths, still hard but slower, brushed her shoulder.

"I love you, Alan," she murmured into his ear as an aftershock rocked her.

"Don't say that," he replied, his voice thick and unreadable as he pulled out of her.

"But—" Suddenly, she felt messy and so cold. How could she face the rest of the pack or the breakfast crowd when she wanted to crawl off and hide in one of her empty fruit crates for the rest of the day?

He stood and cleaned himself with a towel. "You asked for sex. Even that took almost more than I could give."

She grabbed another towel, struggling not to cry again. When she reached for her shorts, he grabbed her wrist. Without a word, he pulled her into his arms and squeezed her against his ribs.

"Shelley." His voice emerged as a whimper, as vulnerable as a newborn pup's.

He did love her. She felt it with wolf knowledge. The wolf also knew he hadn't changed his mind about leaving. At least she had great sex to remember him by. She picked up the mangled orange. Her heart would be in the same shape when he left Moonlight.

Chapter Five

After Shelley headed to the dining room, Alan disinfected the counter. Had they really had wild sex on it? In his fantasies, he'd worried about performing like a bungling idiot since it was his first time, but instinct had taken over. His knees wobbled as if a hurricane had blown through the diner. If he'd known having sex with her would shake him to the soul, he never would have attempted it.

God, she felt and tasted sweeter than oranges. He loved that fruit now. Couldn't wait to drink a big glass of orange juice and devour toast slathered with marmalade. He wanted to spend the rest of his life tasting her breasts.

When she'd exposed her neck to him for the mating bite, he'd been so tempted to complete their union. Aside from avoiding a bond that might keep him here, he was afraid he'd lose control. What if he started biting and the beast couldn't stop? Hurting her would kill his soul.

Why did she have to love him? He was a violent freak, and everyone knew he planned to leave. He closed his eyes, imagining his life in northern Virginia, knowing it would never be the same now.

It would be as empty as hell.

He tied his bandana back on and slipped out the back door to get the rest of the vegetables out of Shelley's truck. He barely had enough time to fire up the grill for the breakfast crowd. In fact, the pack members were starting to arrive. Birds chirped from the nearby woods in the climbing morning heat.

When he reached into her truck for the last crate, full of tomatoes, an expensive looking black sedan pulled up beside him. It was a little too early for tourists. The hairs on the back of his neck prickled. Suddenly, he remembered Shelley's premonition about danger to the pack.

A man in a gray suit stepped out. Definitely not a tourist. Alan's nostrils flared, scanning the air for the man's scent above the tang of tomatoes. *Wolf.* Because he didn't live here, he wasn't familiar with the packs in bordering territories. He sensed this tribe wasn't friendly. A pair of pale-green eyes— ruthless and dead—flicked over him. Alan fought the urge to shiver.

"Excuse me, can you tell me who owns this establishment?"

"Don Shifflett. Why?" Alan asked.

"Is he inside? I'd like to speak with him."

Alan crossed his arms and stood between him and the diner. Shelley was in there, and for some reason, he felt the urge to protect her.

"I'm his son. You can talk to me."

The man hesitated, visibly taking in Alan's bandana, tank top, and jeans. Alan's beast stretched its paws, ready to pounce.

"Graham Linden." The stranger held out his cold hand and the men shook, raising the hackles on Alan's neck even higher. "I'll come right to the point.

We'd like to buy the diner."

Not *I, we*.

Alan raised his chin. "And who is *we*?"

Graham's face twitched with the effort to look neutral and polite. Apparently, Alan didn't appear dressed well enough to rank too highly on his pack's totem pole.

"Lobos Enterprises. We have businesses in various parts of Florida, and we want to expand."

Uneasiness tickled Alan's spine. How did he know the diner was for sale? The pack members would keep the news private, at least for a while, so they'd have first dibs on it. Was a rival pack trying to take over Moonlight's territory? It had happened before, sending its members to live in an orange grove as refugees.

It's not for sale. The words hovered on his lips, but he didn't know why. When the logical part of his brain kicked in, excitement finally gushed through his veins. Wasn't this what he wanted? By the looks of Graham, his outfit had money. Alan could probably get full asking price. Such an easy sale seemed almost too good to be true.

"We're prepared to offer a fair price," the other man said, as if reading his mind. "Our lawyer can have the papers drawn up tomorrow."

Alan's eyes widened. They meant business. He'd never dreamed of such a quick and easy sale. He could return to his job and still have some vacation time left over. But what good would a vacation be without Shelley to enjoy it with? He couldn't help picturing her in a bikini on one of Florida's Gulf-Coast beaches.

The temptation to whip out a pen and lock in a commitment to the deal raced through him. Legally, the diner belonged to his father, not the pack. They'd probably refuse the sale just to spite him, but he thought of Shelley. She worked so hard for the pack. It meant a lot to her. He'd be gone as soon as the ink dried, but she'd be the one living here and dealing with whatever decision he made.

"Come on in, Mr. Linden. I'll give you a tour and some breakfast, on the house."

Might as well let the pack get a sniff of the potential buyer to ease his conscience, but he wasn't going to let anything stand in the way of his quick exit.

***

When Shelley strolled into the dining room with her order pad, she felt naked in front of the pack members who'd arrived for breakfast. Her shirt stuck to her belly, and the scent of sticky orange juice lingered in her hair. Of all days to have to fill in for a sick waitress.

Had Alan really made love to her? The dream she'd carried around for so many years had finally come true. Well, not quite. She dreamed of a wedding and a lifetime spent with her true mate. Their sexy romp on the kitchen counter would be all she'd have. Nevertheless, she'd treasure it for the rest of her days. Especially the intense hug at the end.

Derek sat in his usual spot at the breakfast counter. Since he was the Alpha, he always got served first. Why did Curtis have to sit next to him this morning?

"What'll it be, guys?"

"I'm in the mood for a Spanish omelet today," Derek said, running a hand over black, shower-damp hair. "Throw in a side of bacon and some toast."

She wrote it down in her pad and glanced at Curtis.

"You've had sex." His nostrils flared, and he sniffed the air. "Recently, too. By the smell of you, you didn't even shower afterward. Scabs must have nailed you in the kitchen."

Her pen shook as she held it. "Curtis, this isn't the time or the place. Now, what would you like to eat?"

"Black coffee," he muttered. "I've lost my appetite. Besides, I don't want Scabs cooking my food when his fingers have just been up your cunt."

Derek glared at him. "That'll be enough, Curtis."

Before she turned to go to the kitchen, the Alpha grabbed her wrist. "Based on our last conversation, I didn't think you would mate with Alan."

"I'm sorry." Her shoulders fell. "He didn't bite me, though. Should I have asked your permission?"

Derek released her wrist but fixed her with an Alpha stare. "Not exactly, but we agreed it best he leave again. He'll never go now."

"That's the whole idea," she replied.

"What are you talking about?" Derek asked, frowning more by the second. "It's not like you to put your wants above the good of the pack."

She swept back a hank of hair that had fallen in her face. The day had barely started and it was already off track. Giving Alan her body hadn't changed his mind about leaving, and now the Alpha was disappointed in her. She'd let down her pack. When it came to her man, she couldn't think about anything else.

Shifting would help straighten out her thoughts. Sometimes, a week would go by before she got the urge because she'd been working so hard lately.

Making love had unleashed her wolf. She needed Alan.

"He is good for the pack," she insisted. "He's been wonderful with his father who, as we all know, is a real handful. I'm not happy with the way everyone treated him when he arrived. It was like high school all over again."

"He's a violent son of a bitch." Curtis hammered his fingers on the counter. "I've got the scars to prove it."

She put her hand on her hip. "He hasn't been anything but caring and giving since he arrived."

"His true nature will emerge eventually," Curtis argued. "Once an alcoholic, always an alcoholic. Once violent, always violent."

"Curtis is right to be concerned," Derek agreed. "We all are."

"I told him to stay away from you, Shelley," Curtis added. "Obviously, he didn't listen."

Shelley's heart thudded in her throat as she pictured the prom fight. She would never forgive herself if something like it happened again because of her.

"I forbid you to get into another fight with him." Derek gripped his arm. "The attraction between two mates is often too powerful to resist. You'll understand when you find yours."

"The pack is in danger, but not from Alan. I can feel it." She clenched her order pad. "I don't know how yet, but we'll need him. Soon."

Derek looked her in the eye. "Your intuition has always been spot-on. In the future, though, discuss your concerns with me or at a pack meeting. Given our history, we can't afford to be complacent."

"Will do." She smiled, her shoulders ten pounds

lighter. "I'll go put in your orders."

She couldn't wait to escape to the kitchen and relive Alan's hot, wet tongue burrowing into her navel and teasing her clit. Her panties, barely dry from earlier, grew damp and slick again.

When the bell above the front door jingled, her hackles rose and she dropped her pad and pen. The nameless danger she'd been feeling for days concentrated on the stranger in the suit. No one wore suits around here, and he had the creepiest, deadest eyes she'd ever seen.

The rest of the pack also took notice. Conversations stopped, and several stares drifted toward the man. She picked up what she'd dropped and observed, too.

"The dining room can seat fifty people." Alan set down the crate of tomatoes from her truck and pointed to the ceiling. "The roof was redone only two months ago."

Shelley's pulse dropped to zero. *Oh, Alan. No!* When he'd told her he planned to sell Moonlight Diner, she figured she'd have some time to change his mind. At the least, a member of the pack should have it. None of them even had a chance to review finances and put together an offer.

"Excellent." The stranger gave the room a quick glance. "Show me the kitchen."

Derek stood and glared at the man. "This diner is not for sale."

"The owner's son here tells me it is," the stranger replied, his eyes glittering with warning.

"This is Graham Linden with Lobos Enterprises," Alan said, wiping his sweaty brow. "This is Derek Sawyer, our Al— Our town leader."

"There's been a misunderstanding," Derek said,

glaring at Alan next. "If you want some breakfast, we'll get you a menu."

Shelley hoped not. The mere sight of him made her skin crawl.

"No, thank you." Graham straightened his silk tie. "I'm afraid my boss isn't fond of misunderstandings."

"Is that a threat?" Derek asked.

"We intend to have this diner, one way or another. We prefer to handle the transaction with a civilized sale, but the choice is up to you." He reached inside his jacket and pulled out a card, which he handed Alan. "I'll be in touch."

After he left, pandemonium erupted in the dining room. Derek rose and made calming motions with his hands.

"Who is he?" someone asked.

"By the smell of him, he belongs to the Starwood pack," Derek said. "They're a national outfit, and they like to take over regional packs like ours. They want to rule over all the wolf shifters in the country."

"Oh, no," she whispered, her fingers drifting to her throat.

"Shelley, I'm afraid your intuition was right on the money as usual," the Alpha said. "We're in real danger here."

Alan raised his hands. "If his money is green, what difference does it make? It's just a diner."

"It's not just a diner." Rand, sitting at the end of the breakfast bar, narrowed his silver eyes. "It's central to our pack and symbolic. If they take it, we may as well roll onto our backs and wave our paws in the air."

"I want out," Alan insisted, swiping his fingers across his forehead. "Dad already gave me his permission. Legally, I have the right to sell it."

"No, you don't," Derek shot back. "Like it or not, you're a member of this pack, and I forbid you to sell it to them."

"He's not one of us," Curtis said with a sneer. "Never was."

Alan stalked to the crate of tomatoes he'd set down. Panic swirled in Shelley's belly when she felt the anger billowing off him like smoke. She cringed when he picked up one of the tomatoes and crushed it. Red juice spurted between his fingers, reminding her of blood. A fang lengthened and pierced his lip, drawing the real stuff.

She wished she could kiss it and make it go away before it turned into a scab. If only this whole rotten situation would go away, so they could live a happy, peaceful life together as mates.

Alan grabbed a clean napkin from a nearby place setting and wiped off his messy hands. The gesture reminded her of their lovemaking, sticky with orange juice. Had their sweet joining happened a mere hour ago? It felt as if days had passed.

Please don't prove them right. You're not a violent freak. You're a gentle, caring man.

Shelley must have uttered some sound because his chocolate gaze rested on her. With her eyes, she sent him love and peace, but he looked through her as if she weren't even there.

"I don't want to be here," he said slowly, glaring at the crate. "And you all don't want me here. Something's got to give."

"Look, we've pissed him off," Curtis crowed. "He's more dangerous than Starwood if you ask me."

"Shut up, Curtis. You're not helping," Derek snapped.

Alan's body shook so hard, it appeared to blur—

something she hadn't seen since prom night. With a growl of rage, he picked up the crate and flung it against the wall. She covered her mouth to smother a cry as wood splintered and tomato pulp splattered everywhere.

"Get me the fuck out of this hellhole!" he yelled.

More fangs pushed between his lips, drawing blood and reminding her of a vampire. Hairs sprouted from his arms. He appeared completely out of control. Shelley glanced around the room to make sure no tourists were there to witness the spectacle.

But even if he'd remained calm, he'd still sell them all out without blinking an eye. The Starwood pack seemed serious about its threat. If Alan could walk away when she and their pack were in danger, then he wasn't the man she'd fallen in love with. Did she cling to some schoolgirl fantasy, yearning for the class underdog because she couldn't have him? Maybe she'd matured the least of all of them.

She'd blurted out she loved him too soon. Passion and the instinct of being his mate had popped those careless words into her mouth. Seeing his patience and caring for his difficult father made her feelings for him grow, but he had a point. They really didn't know each other very well.

"Hey, Scabs!" Triumph glittered in Curtis's eyes as he leaned back in his seat like a spectator at a ball game. "You won't get much money for the place if you trash it."

Derek and Rand bolted out of their seats and looped their arms through Alan's. They lifted him off his feet while he thrashed and kicked the air like a lunatic. They almost lost their grip on him when he shifted into wolf form.

Except for the bare patches, his reddish-brown

hackles vibrated from neck to tail. Violent chills racked Shelley's body when his foaming jaws snapped the air, seeking flesh to bite. Unable to watch anymore, she looked down, half expecting to see the pink silk of her prom dress instead of denim shorts.

Liana Aquino, a refugee from another pack and part-time waitress, grabbed a roll of paper towels and the dishrag left behind on the breakfast counter to clean up the mess. Shelley should help her, but her body had frozen into a rock.

She'd worked so hard to raise those tomatoes—starting them from seeds in the greenhouse, fighting pests organically, picking, packing, and hauling them. Seeing the satisfaction on the faces of the diner's customers as they ate Don's spaghetti sauce or omelets made her efforts worthwhile.

But the man she supposedly loved had destroyed her harvest in a blink of an eye. If he quarreled with her, would he throw her against the wall, too? After what she'd witnessed, she wouldn't put it past him.

When she could finally move her muscles, she dropped her order pad and ran outside. Alan's loss of control had to be contagious because she rushed behind the building, dropped to all fours, and shifted. Never mind cleaning up his mess, prepping sandwich fixings for lunch, or wondering if her clothes would still be there when she got back. All she wanted to do was get away from him because he was right.

He *was* a freak!

Chapter Six

When Shelley bounded out the door, Alan loosed a howl that shook the rafters. He hadn't seen her shift but knew with a mate's instinct she had. Every cell in his body screamed for him to follow her.

Brett looked out the window. "Customers are coming."

"Calm down." Derek gave Alan a gentle shake. "Shift back now or pretend you're my dog."

Alan went limp all at once, reverting to his human form. *Holy hell!* What had he done? Luckily, he'd simply thrown some tomatoes and not tried to choke anyone, but he'd lost control. What if he'd killed a tourist? He had to get out of Florida—quick. If he ended up in jail, he wouldn't have a normal life left to return to.

"Sorry," he muttered while Rand helped him into his clothes. "I don't know what got into me."

"We'll figure something out," Derek said.

Alan's feet still itched with the urge to follow his mate and calm her down, but why bother? He couldn't erase the spectacle he'd created. It was for the best. Now that she'd seen his true colors again, she wouldn't try to keep him here anymore. Instead of relief, a yawning emptiness opened inside him.

He cleared his throat, which was raw from screaming and howling. "I'll start on breakfast."

"I'll send someone in to help you."

Alan held up a hand. "No. I need to be alone."

When Shelley returned, and he knew she would out of duty, they needed to talk. Sure enough, she rushed in fifteen minutes later with a handful of breakfast orders. By then, the grill was hot, and he'd whipped up a bowl full of pancake batter.

For now, cooking channeled his jagged energy. For some strange reason, it felt better today than sitting at a boring keyboard. Filling people's stomachs, giving them strength and sustenance, was more primal than a bunch of silly computers people had managed to live without for centuries.

Her face remained expressionless as she handed him the breakfast orders like a business colleague at the office, but her eyes were red. Had she been crying? When he picked up a tomato for an omelet, their gazes dropped to it then locked with each other's. The tiny flinch that ran through her— flickering in her eyes and rippling her shoulders— flayed his heart.

"Should I duck?" she asked.

"I'm sorry, Shelley." His throat was still so raw he felt as if he'd caught a bad cold. "I didn't mean to ruin your tomatoes."

Remembering the big red stain on the wall made him shiver. Had he really done that? In front of the whole pack, no less. Curtis had probably enjoyed the scene more than the movies.

"It's all right," she said, sounding as expressionless as she looked. "You couldn't help it."

He broke open an egg on the edge of a steel bowl.

"At least now you see what I really am and why I have to leave."

She poured some pancake batter onto the grill, forming circles as round as her breasts. The woman was way too damn perfect for a freak like him.

"I wish—" She bit her knuckle.

The egg slid onto the counter, instead of into the bowl. He couldn't even scramble a lousy egg without screwing it up. Part of him ached to pretend he could be her mate. That he could change. Shifting must have eased her fear because her eyes were soft with hope.

Was she crazy? How could she witness the violent freak at its worst and look at him as if she still cared and saw the best in him?

"Don't wish," he said, hardening his voice. "And for God's sake, don't love me. I'm not even capable of returning it."

She flinched again but nodded. "Moonlight pack is my family and home. All I ask is that you think of the pack before selling out."

Irritation prickled his spine, but it felt nothing like what he'd experienced earlier. His wolf's instinct told him he'd never hurt her, but his logical mind wasn't so sure.

"I *am* thinking of the pack." He scooped up the raw egg and dumped it onto the sizzling grill. "I'm a danger to them and you. If you don't believe it, you're hopelessly naive."

Her bottom lip trembled, and she shrank from him. Good. It meant he was finally getting through to her.

He grabbed the spatula from her limp hand. "If selling to Starwood gets me out of here the fastest, then I'm going to do it."

The sooner she got it through her head they weren't right for each other, the better. Having sex with her had been a mistake. Even though they hadn't done the mating bond, the act had connected them. From now on, he needed to keep her at a distance no matter how much it ripped him apart.

***

When the breakfast rush died down, Alan wiped the grease from his hands with a rag. Luckily, it had been so busy Shelley hadn't said another word to him. She'd left fifteen minutes ago to return to her farm, and Liana had taken over waiting tables.

He headed for the door, hoping to find someone to fill in for him, too, so he could check on his father. They also had to discuss Starwood's offer. After this morning's outburst, he needed to be with kin.

In the dining room, several pack members gathered around a large round table. They huddled forward like a football team and spoke in low voices so the tourists wouldn't overhear them. Even though it made his belly lurch, he stepped toward them.

"Can someone take over in the kitchen for a while?" Alan asked. "I need to check on Dad."

"Sure." Charlie Aquino, a friend of the pack, sipped the coffee he stopped by for so often. "We've been discussing the diner, trying to find a solution to suit everybody."

Including him? Alan blinked. Maybe he'd underestimated them. Then again, Curtis was gone. Earlier, Derek could have punished him but had only restrained him. If he wanted an Alpha in his life, which he didn't, he probably wouldn't find a better one.

How would it feel to be part of the Starwood pack? It seemed to be a businesslike outfit similar to his corporate life. Just get the job done with no strong attachments. Moonlight was more like family. Not being a part of it was worse than being alone.

"I'll buy it myself if I have to," Derek said, draining the rest of his coffee. "Better yet, why don't a group of us take ownership of it? We can share the expense, labor, and profits."

"Good idea," Rand said. "Count me in."

"Liana and I are in, too." Charlie looked at his wife. "Right, babe?"

"Of course," she replied with a smile.

"As long as the diner gets sold, I'm a happy camper," Alan said. "All I want to do is go home and get out of your hair."

"Believe it or not, we all want the same thing," Derek declared.

"I'll discuss it with Dad this afternoon," Alan offered. Maybe pack mentality was finally sinking into his brain because the need for consensus circulated through his blood.

When he headed to the parking lot, though, he found Dad shuffling toward the front door on the sturdy arm of Rita, his caregiver. He wore baggy sweatpants and a pajama top.

Alan frowned at him. "What are you doing here?"

The Hispanic woman shot him a helpless look. "He wouldn't take no for an answer."

"I need to be in my diner," the older man practically growled. "Otherwise, you might as well bury my carcass right now."

Alan's stomach dropped. If he sold the diner, especially to another pack, it wouldn't be his father's territory anymore. Getting him back to the house probably wouldn't be any easier. After his outburst, he didn't have the strength to argue.

"Let's get him settled in the storeroom. He and I need to talk alone."

Relief flooded Rita's dark eyes. From what Shelley had told him, Alan knew she was a refugee from another pack who'd joined theirs after he'd left. Judging by the wary expression on her cinnamon-hued face, she knew about his violent reputation.

"Sure." She helped Don up the stoop. "Meanwhile, I can make a grocery run."

In the storeroom, Alan cut the steak and cheese sub he'd hastily fried up and gave his father half.

"I received an offer for the diner this morning."

Dad's grizzled eyebrows rose. "So soon? Who from?"

When Alan told him about Graham from the Starwood pack, he nearly choked on his sub.

"You mean you'd sell my heritage to a rival pack? What kind of son are you?"

"I have a job to return to." Alan kept his voice calm, fighting the irritation prickling across his skin. "The pack proposed buying it as a group, but that could be drawn out and complicated. The quicker and cleaner the sale, the better."

"I don't want to sell it."

"What!" Alan dropped his sub and the meat inside spilled out on the counter. "But you agreed."

"I changed my mind. I have a better idea."

"Can't wait to hear it," Alan said, crossing his arms.

"I want you to run it."

He let out a choked laugh. "No way. I hate cooking."

Having Shelley pressed close to his side making

pancakes earlier hadn't been too painful, though. Her presence calmed him in a way he couldn't explain.

Don picked a piece of onion out of his beard. "So hire a cook."

Why was everyone so determined to keep him here? Okay, the pack wasn't, but Shelley and Dad— the only people who mattered to him—were.

"You know I have a life to get back to."

"Oh, yes, your wonderful life." Dad's gaze drifted to the ceiling. "Why you'd rather freeze your balls off up there alone and sit in front of a computer all day is beyond me."

Alan picked up his sub meat and downed it in a couple of bites. He was a monster, so he may as well eat like one.

"You weren't here earlier when I threw a crate of tomatoes against the wall." Sweat beaded across his brow from the mere thought of it. "I was completely out of control. Shelley and most of the pack saw it."

"You could learn to control the beast like I did," the old man shot back.

"Yeah, right." Alan picked the cheese out of his bread and gulped it. "After I kill a few people along the way."

Don waved a greasy hand. "Young people have no patience. A man belongs with his mate."

"That happily-ever-after shit is for normal men and shifters."

Dad set down his half-eaten sandwich. "Where do you think you came from? An alien spaceship? I had a woman once."

An image of Alan's mother flashed through his mind. She'd died when he was six from an illness. He remembered her gentleness the most. How she dabbed his runny nose when he was sick. Pulled his boots on before he went out into the rain. Best of all, how she snuggled with him before he went to sleep at night, reading him stories.

Shelley was gentle. Too much for her own good. He could easily picture her raising his pups.

"Weren't you afraid you'd hurt her?"

"At first." Don chuckled. "Let me tell you, we had some barn-burnin' arguments, but I never harmed one hair on her head. Not even close."

Alan popped an onion slice into his mouth, chewing it carefully instead of swallowing it whole. He suspected he'd never hurt Shelley, either, but he couldn't trust a hunch. He stood, walked to the window, and gazed at the woods. When the black sedan had pulled up, he'd been so ready to sell. He wasn't the same man he'd been this morning. Every minute he stayed in this place, the harder it became to leave.

"She's better off without me," he said. "I've told her so several times."

"So, you're going to leave her here to rot with no mate or children of her own?"

Alan gripped the windowsill. "I'm keeping her safe."

"Why don't you let her take care of herself instead of deciding everything for her? Hell, she takes care of everybody else around here."

"She's pretty amazing," Alan agreed. "I don't know how she finds time to do charity work on top of farming and helping out in the diner."

"That's not the half of it. When any of the pack children are sick, she visits them or sends them little gifts to cheer them up. And when her neighbor's barn blew down during the last hurricane, there she was, hauling his animals to her farm to care for them.

Reminded me of Noah's Ark."

Wow. She'd come a long way from the spoiled beauty queen of his high school days.

"The point is," Don continued after a slow belch, "you're too bossy. You treat me like a child, too."

"If I'm so screwed up," Alan asked, turning to glare at his father, "why are you so determined to make me stay?"

"Because there's hope for you. I can't die in peace until I get you straightened out."

"Now who's treating the other like a child?"

"You are a good cook, you know." Don wiped his greasy lips and belched again. "Getting back to the woman...do you love her?"

Did he? The wolf inside him howled in reply as he sat down again and munched another slice of onion. After witnessing him throw a tomato crate against the wall, most women would have told him to stay the hell away. Shelley wasn't most women. She saw the good in him no matter what. Not to mention her hard work and selflessness. The pack would probably fall apart if it weren't for her. Moonlight Diner sure would have.

"Yes." His answer emerged in a hoarse whisper. "But it doesn't change anything."

Don sagged before his eyes, leaning on his elbows as he hunched over the table.

Heart thudding, Alan rushed to his side and gave his shoulder a gentle shake. "Are you okay?"

"I'll live, today." Dad blinked tired-looking eyes. "Talked myself out of breath."

"You need to stop worrying about me." Alan stacked their dirty plates. "I'll drive you home so you can rest."

Dad nodded, wheezing as he stood. "Since you

don't like anything I've proposed today, I'll keep it simple and give you one request."

"Which is?" Alan slid his arm under Dad's armpit and guided him toward the door.

"If you must sell the diner, don't do it until I'm gone. Not even to the pack."

Alan squeezed his eyes shut. The man was impossible. "Why?"

The old man, frail and thin on his arm, growled like the majestic wolf he'd always been. "Because I said so."

Alan knew what he was up to. He figured if his son stayed long enough, he'd never leave. Even more reason to get out of here. His logical mind listed the things he needed to do.

Get Dad home and into bed. Call Graham Linden and tell him the diner wasn't for sale, ever. Notify the pack of Dad's request. Most importantly, call the airline because his ass was flying out of here tomorrow morning no matter what. Let the pack members run the diner like they had before he'd shown up. It would be good practice for when they finally owned it.

Before he left, though, he needed Shelley to know he loved her. His stomach dropped to his feet as if he stood inside an elevator with a snapped cable. For some reason, revealing his feelings scared him worse than losing control of his beast.

***

Shelley rushed into the diner around three in the afternoon to make pies for dessert. Farming chores, it seemed, were never done, but they'd kept her mind off Alan. If he didn't want to be with her, she couldn't change his mind. She was tired of throwing herself at him and looking like an idiot. Even though she didn't believe for one minute his uncontrollable temper would ever harm her, she appreciated his concern.

She couldn't control the diner sale, either. For the first time since he'd arrived, she looked forward to watching him leave. Back to the life that was more important to him than her and the pack. Letting him go felt better than a breath of fresh breeze on a humid afternoon.

Barbara cornered her before she reached the kitchen. "Good news. Scabs has decided not to sell the place to the Starwood pack."

"Please don't call him that." Shelley's heart fluttered along with her hands. "Never mind. What is he going to do with it? Is he here?"

"He's going to sell it to the pack, but the old man requested we wait until he passes away."

"That's wonderful!" Shelley exclaimed. "I want to be one of the owners. We could redecorate."

Maybe she'd written Alan off too soon, but she refused to get her hopes up about a relationship. He'd shot her down too many times. She'd settle for his helping the pack, which was a lot more important than her selfish desires.

"You read my mind, girlfriend." Barbara flung her hand toward the faded, red-checked curtains and dark paneling that looked like something from the 70s. "Men have no taste. This place needs a serious renovation."

When Shelley took a step toward the kitchen, Barbara handed her a sealed envelope. "Oh, and he asked me to give you this."

Having no idea what it could be, she broke a nail ripping into it. The small envelope, made of heavy paper, reminded her of the ill-fated prom invitation and Barbara's role in it.

Was Alan paying her back for it? Did he keep pushing her away because he could never forgive her for that miserable night?

Her fingers trembled as she pulled out the card.

I could write another poem because there are so many in my heart, but I'll keep it simple.

You are cordially invited to Don's cottage at 7 pm for a romantic, home-cooked dinner.

Go home and get some rest. The pack will fill in for us at the diner tonight.

Alan

She read it again and two more times. Alan planned to cook her dinner? Why? She lifted her knuckles to her mouth and bit down. Had he changed his mind about their relationship? Or chosen this way of saying good-bye? Butterflies did an aerial show in her stomach. To find out, she'd have to show up.

Barbara leaned closer. "Well, what does it say?"

Since the other woman had been giving her the cold shoulder since Alan arrived, Shelley figured sharing might heal the friendship. "Alan is cooking me a romantic dinner."

"Sounds serious." Barbara wrinkled her nose. "I heard you slept with him."

Familiar peer pressure jabbed Shelley in the spine. "So?"

"So, you should've married Curtis. He's gorgeous and sane."

Shelley put a hand on her hip. "Alan has a genetic mutation. He's not insane."

"Think twice." Barbara pointed a finger at her. "Or

you might end up in the hospital from one of his spastic fits. Or with a bunch of mutated pups even freakier than he is."

"I don't like your attitude," Shelley bit out.

"Hey, I'm just trying to be a friend."

"Well, I don't need friends like you! Not anymore." After turning on her heel, she marched out.

Chapter Seven

Alan whistled a tune as he opened the front door of his father's house at dusk. He'd called Graham to tell him he wasn't selling the diner. The man had said he was very sorry to hear it and to contact him when he reconsidered. Not *if* he reconsidered but *when*. Sore loser. He'd find something else to buy and get over it.

Better still, a plane to Dulles leaving late tomorrow morning had a seat with his name on it.

Who was he kidding? The reason he whistled was tonight's date. He couldn't give Shelley a relationship, but he could enjoy a real date like a normal man. The crotch of his jeans tightened as he anticipated making slow, sweet love to her. Maybe it would help him get through his celibate future. He didn't want the beast rutting her on the kitchen counter to be her only memory of him, either.

And, hard as it was, he'd tell her he loved her. She knew he'd leave sooner or later, so it couldn't hurt.

Rita met him at the door. The sight of her wide eyes and mouth pulled down at the corners shot a bolt of adrenaline through him.

"What's happened to Dad?"

Please tell me he hasn't passed yet. Today, they'd

shared the best conversation of their lives. When the bad news finally came, he wanted to get a phone call or an email, not be here in person. That would be too close. Too unbearable.

"He's fine now," Rita said in her usual calm voice.

When he glanced down at the bloody tissues in her hand, his heart shot into overdrive. The brownish-red streak on her orange pants must be blood, too.

"What the hell?"

"Oh, this?" She looked down. "Just a nosebleed. He, eh, had some visitors earlier."

"Pack members?"

"Not from our pack. Two men in suits. One of them was named Graham something or other." She handed him a card from the counter. It looked exactly like the one he already had. Same dude, all right.

Holy orange pulp. Starwood had come here? To threaten a sick old man? He bounded toward his father's bedroom.

"From now on, no one is allowed in the house unless they're from our pack," he barked out. "Understood?"

"Yes, sir." Her eyes widened even more as she took a step back. "Will you be home the rest of the evening? Should I cook dinner?"

Alan nodded. "Fix something special. I'm having a date over."

"I'll set out some candles," she replied, finally smiling. "Sounds like *amour* is in the air."

It was, but Starwood had ruined the mood of his date before it had even begun. He still needed to talk to Shelley, though. She needed to know what the Moonlight pack was up against.

He stepped into Dad's bedroom and gently closed the door behind him. A bit of dried blood clung to a skin crevice at the end of the man's nose as he lay in bed. It made his face look paler and his hair whiter.

Alan clenched his fists. "What the hell happened?"

"Nothing. Now sit down and calm yourself before you strain something."

Still crabby. A good sign. Alan turned down the talk show on the small TV, dragged a chair closer to the bed, and sat.

"A couple of dudes in fancy suits came over, asking me to sign some papers." He wrinkled his nose. "Well, first they asked. Then they demanded."

Cold sweat bloomed across Alan's skin, and the smell of pork chops drifting in from the kitchen made him nauseous. He should have been here to protect him.

He wiped his forehead. "Did you sign?"

"Hell no, I didn't sign those fool papers." Don gripped the edge of the sheet, which lay neatly folded across his chest. "They'd have to kill me first."

"Your safety is more important than a restaurant." Alan waved a hand. "What did you do?"

"You know how prone I am to nosebleeds." Dad held up his index finger, tipped by a yellowed fingernail. "I just stuck this up my nose and brought one on. Bled all over those fancy papers."

His pajama top was spotless, though. Rita must have changed his clothes.

The strain in Alan's chest gushed out in a laugh. "You're something else."

But his beast stirred, squeezing his muscles— preparing him for battle? The Starwood pack had gone too far.

"Did they hurt you?"

"They didn't lay a hand on me." Dad's brows bristled, and the brass bed squeaked as he pumped a fist in the air. "They knew better than to try."

But they were both aware a sick, aged wolf would be no match for two younger, stronger ones.

"And I told them if they came back with more papers, I'd throw up on 'em and their suits, too."

Alan stood and cracked his knuckles. "There won't be a next time."

Don's nose twitched. "I smell fried pork chops and corn bread."

"I'll have Rita bring you a tray so you can stay in bed." Alan looked down at his feet. "Shelley is, uh, coming over for dinner."

"Is she now?" Dad grinned. "My advice today must have gotten into that thick skull of yours."

"It's not what you think. I plan to tell her how I feel, like you suggested, but mainly I'm going to say good-bye."

"Good-bye?" Don's voice softened to a whisper. "Sounds like you're planning to leave soon."

Alan squeezed his hand but couldn't look at him. "My plane leaves tomorrow, but don't worry. You'll be safe. I promise."

But how could he guarantee his words? He was leaving. No sweat. Derek and Rand owned The Defenders, a private security agency. He'd hire them to guard his father's home around the clock. Starwood would probably lose interest and move on to greener pastures soon, anyway.

He glanced at his watch. Since Rita was cooking, he had time to pack before dinner. How strange. The one thing he'd looked forward to since the night he arrived now felt about as appealing as an old dog turd.

***

Shelley ran a hand through her hair after ringing Don's doorbell. It felt weird not to wear the usual rubber band. Next, she smoothed the rose-colored dress she wore. It had flowing lines and spaghetti straps. She'd even worn high-heeled sandals. When was the last time she'd dressed up? She spent so much time farming and handling food she probably smelled like a turnip.

Alan answered the door in dark jeans and a long-sleeved striped shirt. He still wore his black bandana, though. His melted-chocolate eyes took her in from head to toe.

"Come in, my lady." Bowing, he held out a hand.

"I like the formality," she said as she clasped it. "You clean up pretty nice, Alan."

The wolf in her was too busy sniffing his sexy scent to inspect his clothes too closely, though.

He whistled. "So do you."

She stepped inside, and her stomach did a little flip when she realized they were alone.

"Where's Don?" she asked.

"Asleep," he said, showing her to a walnut-brown dining room table.

A couple of candles burned from brass holders centered on lace doilies. Her tired feet ached to kick off her shoes and sink into the gold shag carpet. The old-fashioned room sounded blissfully quiet after the clatter of the diner.

Her stomach growled as several appetites in her blossomed at once. "Something smells good."

"I wish I could take the credit, but Rita whipped something up before she left."

She didn't care if the governor of Florida had prepared the meal. Tonight, she wanted only Alan, wherever and however she could get him. Heat banked in her belly like a persistent fog as they filled their plates at the stove.

After they sat down, she took a few bites. The pork chops tasted delicious, but excitement kept her from savoring them properly.

"This is a wonderful surprise." She gazed at the candle flame in front of her. "I'm almost afraid to ask, but what's the occasion?"

When he wiped some olive oil from his mouth, she itched to do it for him with her tongue. Realizing he did it to delay his answer cooled her ardor.

"One reason is to apologize to you for the way I acted this morning, ruining your tomatoes. Hang on a second."

She frowned when he jumped up to visit the refrigerator. He sure acted mysterious tonight. With great solemnity, he brought back a tomato with a heart carved into it and set it in front of her.

After raising her fingers to her mouth, she laughed through them. "Oh, Alan."

His dark eyes grew serious. "I don't want to be the cliché violent guy who apologizes to his woman and promises he'll never do it again. So, I'm just saying I'm sorry."

"Thank you." She let her hand rest on his across the table. "But don't worry about it. You didn't exactly beat me up."

"You're my mate. I would never hurt you," he said quietly as a single shiver shook his shoulders. "At least I hope I wouldn't."

"What's the other reason?"

When he looked down at his lap, her heart landed on her high-heeled shoes like a dead fish. She should have known a romantic dinner would be too good to be true.

"You're leaving, aren't you?" she asked. "When?"

His gaze rose and locked onto hers. "Tomorrow."

Tomorrow. She'd never hated a word so much. It struck her in the chest with the force of a hammer. A wooden clock ticked from the wall, marking what little time they had left.

"So, this is good-bye."

He nodded. "But we have tonight. Shelley, there are so many things I need to say to you."

She wasn't sure she could stand to hear them, but she couldn't bear to leave yet.

"I'm going to hire The Defenders to have someone guard Dad. Starwood sent two goons over here today to pressure him to sell the diner. One of them was the same guy I turned down."

"Oh, no." What a bittersweet romantic dinner. Plenty of romance but also a boatload of bad news to go along with it. "He didn't, did he?"

"Luckily, no."

"My afternoon wasn't so great, either," she said. "Barbara and I aren't friends anymore."

His brow creased. "Because of me?"

"It was a long time coming." She shrugged. "I don't care what she thinks anymore about my taste in men."

"Maybe she'll grow up someday, like you."

When she rose to help him clear the plates, he held up his hand. "You're off duty tonight."

He returned to the table, grasped her bare shoulders, and rubbed lazy circles on them. His touch felt so good she closed her eyes and sighed.

"You have such pretty shoulders," he murmured. "Soft but strong. You'd never know by looking at them how much weight they carry in the pack."

"Thank you, Alan. I think you have the makings for another poem in there somewhere."

"We'll see." He flashed her a teasing grin. "I'd play some music, but I'm afraid it would wake Dad. Will you pretend dance with me?"

"Sure."

While his arms slid around her waist, she wrapped hers around his upper back, drinking in the thick cotton of his shirt and his scent. Without words, they hugged each other's bodies tight as they swayed to a silent beat.

The close physical contact made her eyes burn. How could she say good-bye to him now? Ever? He'd only been here a few days, and he already felt like part of her soul. Her love. Her mate. Her everything. And she was going to lose him before she'd even had him.

His bandana tickled her face when he leaned his forehead against hers. His breath, slow and warm, brushed her cheek. It felt so right to be this close to him, she melted faster than a piece of key lime pie in the sun.

"Shelley, I— Oh, hell."

"What are you trying to say, Alan?" she whispered.

"Before I leave, I want you to know something."

They both spoke quietly so they wouldn't wake his father. Alan was finally laying his soul bare to her— something that had never happened before and probably never would again. She didn't care if a hurricane ripped through the cottage. Nothing had better ruin this rare moment.

"Do you need to write another poem?" she teased. "What is it already?"

"Nothing much." He looked down at his shoes. "I just...I love you, Shelley."

A tremor rippled through her arms, locking him closer. Those were the best words she'd heard all day. Knowing how hard it had been for him to say them made them more precious. They still rocked to an unheard beat, in the perfect unison only mates could achieve.

She pressed her cheek against his. "Oh, Alan. You know how I feel about you, too."

"Don't. I don't deserve it." He shook his head, making the tied ends of his bandana bounce. "I'm a violent freak."

"No, you're not," she said, glaring into his eyes while she gripped his hands. "Don't ever say that again."

"Why, angel? Why?" He brushed her chin with his index finger. "Why do you keep believing in me when nobody else does? When I don't even believe in myself?"

"Because you have two men inside." She poked a finger to his breastbone. "You only see the bad one, but I see the tender boy who writes beautiful poems."

His eyes softened, widening to two dark pools of fire, which threatened to swallow her up.

"But I'm so hard and you're so soft," he argued. "What do you see in me?"

"You're soft, too, on the inside," she said, wondering where the words came from as she said them. "Maybe you're hard on the outside because you're so soft inside."

He pressed his rigid pelvis against her. "Soft? Are you sure?"

"Be serious." She sighed as her core melted, needing him inside her more than her lungs needed oxygen. "You're like...a hidden moon. Everyone else sees the clouds, but I see the light behind them."

His mouth twisted up in a half-grin. "You've got me all figured out, huh?"

As they swayed in silence, his liquid gaze caressed her face and drifted over her collarbones, strong and hot as a physical touch. The skin under her confining panties swelled and heated up. As they moved, the slinky fabric of the dress teased her, making her crave his touch.

"Any other particular reason you invited me here?" she asked.

"Yeah, one more."

Her breath caught as he ran a finger down the bodice opening of her dress. Because she hadn't worn a bra, her stiff nipples stretched the fabric. But, damn him, he wouldn't touch them. Instead, his teasing strokes stayed near the opening, studying the curves of her breasts from the sides and bottoms.

He shot her a serious look. "Are you aware you have the most perfect breasts in the universe?"

She laughed, but desire quickly dissolved her humor. While staring into his eyes, she slid two fingers up his cheek and hooked them under the bandana, lifting it off.

"Oh, you shouldn't have done that," he said, shooting her a wicked little smile.

She tossed it to the floor. "Why not?"

In reply, he pressed a strong palm to her buttocks and squeezed. She must have turned into an orange because hot juices dripped into her panties as a result. Next, he pressed a scalding hot kiss to the tender spot where her neck met her shoulder. Her fingers curled around the back of his collar as he sucked and licked the tender skin.

Her heels wobbled in the carpet as he worked his mouth in a slow, lazy path up her neck, across her cheek, and finally to her parted lips. Every inch or so, he stopped to press hot, moist kisses to her skin with his deliciously full lips. Sometimes he sucked a little. Other times, he swiped with the tip of his tongue.

"Alan." The word spilled out of her mouth as a half-plea, half-demand.

"Come on." He grasped her hand and led her to the couch. "The last reason I invited you here was to make sweet love to you."

"You mean you didn't enjoy banging me on the counter at the diner?"

"Hell, yeah, I enjoyed it," he said, shooting her his sexy, boyish smile. "But that was just hot sex. My first time, too."

Her eyebrows shot up. She was his first? His only? She wished she could say the same about him. If she hadn't played games in high school, they'd probably be married by now instead of parting.

"You sure seemed to know what you were doing," she said.

"I guess I learned a few things from watching the adult channel on cable." He brushed back a lock of her hair. "The point is you deserve better. Lie down."

Her pulse throbbed all the way down to her toes as she kicked off her sandals and lay on her back on the big, velveteen sofa. He pulled up the skirt of her dress, but she was too lost in his kiss to pay attention. The sound of rustling clothes and fast, soft breaths surrounded them. He whispered her name while he parted her thighs with warm fingers. Tangling in her panties. Pulling them down, too.

She unbuttoned his shirt, reaching inside to explore the hot planes of his chest along the way.

"What if your father wakes up?" she asked when she reached the last button.

"He won't." All the same, he tugged the red-white-and-blue afghan from the back of the couch and covered them with it.

When he unzipped his fly, her nerves were so taut it sounded like cannon fire in the quiet room. Her slit wept, needing her mate's body and soul. Too eager to wait, she guided him inside, leaving behind a layer of his silky wetness on her fingertips. While he kissed her with exquisite gentleness, she stroked his bare scalp. It was smooth and surprisingly soft. While he eased into her depths, he groaned softly into her mouth.

"Alan," she half-whispered, half-moaned. While the couch embraced her from behind, she gripped his shoulders and embraced him with her thighs, giving him everything—her eager body, her fast-beating heart, and her future.

So precious. So brief. The best moments of her life. If only she could lock them into a box like a pair of earrings and enjoy them later, after he was gone.

His mouth pulled away from hers, leaving her lips cold. "What's the matter?"

"I'm thinking about tomorrow. I really don't like that word."

He toyed with her bottom lip and pressed a kiss onto it while he slid deep. "Tomorrow doesn't exist tonight."

She arched her back, inviting him even farther into her core and squeezing him like a possessive mate.

He winced. "Damn, Shelley. Keep doing that and I'm going come."

"Alan?"

"Uh-huh?" He whistled out a slow breath as she locked her legs around him and dug her heels into his taut buttocks.

"The mating bond," she said, panting. "This time. Please."

He slid his hands under her buttocks, still stroking slowly enough to make her lose her mind.

"You know I want to, but I can't," he whispered.

She swallowed. "I won't ask you to stay. I promise."

"I'm sorry, Shelley." He closed his eyes and dropped his head. "It wouldn't be right."

Why did he have to be so honorable? But he still brought his generous mouth to her neck, tasting and probing with his tongue, as if he also wondered what it would be like to consummate their bond. She squirmed under him, her juices soaking his hard flesh, and probably the couch cushion beneath her.

He reared back, displaying his sexy bare chest. She slid her palms over it—his hot sweat, muscles, and ribs—while he rotated his hips, hugging her from the inside out and setting off sensations so intense they nearly paralyzed her. *My mate*, the wolf in her declared.

When he gazed at her, he told her with his eyes he was about to come. After dropping her hands from his chest, she dug her nails into the base of his spine, driving him into her—harder, deeper, faster. So hard his torso dropped, crushing her chest. The sudden movement made her abdomen clench. Feeling so ripped apart she didn't know if she was alive or dead, she screamed into his shoulder.

He dragged in a huge breath that ended on her name as his seed exploded inside her. Each aftershock of his set off one in her and vice versa as their bodies echoed each other. She roved her hands over him while they rested, their hearts thudding in unison. Memorizing the curve of his skull here and the slope of his shoulder there. Most of all, his deep-brown chocolate eyes as he gazed at her and caressed an exposed breast.

When he finally spoke, his voice sounded hoarse. "Love hurts, doesn't it?"

She traced the outline of his ear, forcing back the heavy wall of heat building behind her eyes. "Yes, it does, Alan, but in a good way. At least with us."

While the spell of their incredible lovemaking slowly evaporated around them, the wolf in her tuned into her surroundings. She peeped over the back of the couch, hoping she wouldn't find his father standing there watching.

A slight breeze wafted in from the window overlooking the orange grove. The wolf in her sniffed.

"Do you smell smoke?"

"Hmm?" Alan yawned and stretched as he sat up. "Yeah, I wonder—"

Straightening her dress, she scrambled off the couch and rushed toward the window. In the distance, she spotted a reddish glow.

"My orange grove. Oh God, Alan! It's on fire!"

Chapter Eight

"I've got to go," Shelley said over her shoulder as she raced toward the front door.

Alan grabbed her arm. "You're not rushing into that fire."

"My oranges," she cried. "I've got to—"

"No." Squeezing her squirming arm, he drew her closer. "First, I'm going to call the pack. Make sure they know. Find someone to guard Dad. Then we'll go."

"That'll take forever." The ferocity in her usually gentle hazel eyes reminded him she was a wolf. "The grove will be burned by then."

He jerked his head toward the door. "I can't leave him, and I'm not letting you head into a fire by yourself."

"I'm a farmer, for God's sake, not helpless." She dug short but sharp nails into his forearm. "I'll be careful."

"No way. Fire kills and whoever set it may still be out there."

He dragged her toward the phone and picked it up with his free hand. Luckily, Dad had their Alpha on speed dial. The movement gave Shelley enough leverage to break free of him.

"Shelley!" His raised voice echoed inside the room. "As your mate, I forbid you to walk out that door without me."

She gripped the doorknob and planted her other hand on her hip. "You're not my mate. You refused to bond, remember?"

Oh, yeah. Crap.

When Derek answered, Alan put the phone on speaker so Shelley could hear. His tongue tripped over itself as he tried to explain everything.

"Do not let her go alone," the Alpha said. "I'll send someone over to guard your father. Is the fire threatening the house?"

Alan glanced out the window, his heart thundering in his ears. "Unless a stray spark blows over here, I don't think so."

"I'm going to get those old clothes from the truck and wet them down while we wait." She opened the door. "I need to call Mom, too, and make sure she's okay. I'll be right back. I promise."

"Okay. I'm glad you obey your Alpha, at least." He picked up his bandana off the floor and tied it around his head again.

"I obey my mate, too," she said. "I don't need a bite to prove you're mine."

Warmth spread through his chest. Well, he did. With everything happening, he couldn't sink his teeth into her neck fast enough. While she handled the clothes they'd wear, he hooked up the hose and wet down the roof as a precaution.

After Alan put on the wet clothes, Dad peered out of his bedroom. Frowning and rumple-haired, he looked like a bear that had been pulled out of hibernation before spring.

"I smell smoke," he said, nose twitching. "What the hell is going on?"

"The orange grove is burning," Shelley said, gripping the windowsill.

Alan swallowed, trying not to notice how hot she looked in a wet T-shirt with no bra. Headlights swept across the driveway.

"That must be the guy Derek sent." He glanced at his father. "He's going to stay with you until we return."

"Oh, that won't be necessary," Don said. "I'm going with you."

"Are you out of your mind?" Alan gripped his head, ready to pull his bandana off again. "You'd only be in the way."

Dad's head drooped. "Thanks a lot."

"Lock him up if you have to," Alan told the guard when he walked in. "Keep him safe."

He'd have his hands full protecting his mate. His gut twisted at the thought of leaving his father alone even for a couple of hours. How could he leave him for good tomorrow?

He couldn't face that day yet. Wasn't even sure he could get through tonight.

Hand in hand, he and Shelley ran out the door.

"Let's take my truck," she said.

"I'll drive."

She shot him a brief grin as she slid into the passenger seat. "You're awfully alpha."

With his heart in his throat, he drove toward the flames. If he'd just arrived from Virginia, the fire wouldn't even faze him. Why should he care? He hadn't even known this place existed. Now, he cared enough to battle the flames himself.

A siren split the air, and red flashing lights

competed with the glow of the flames. Alan pulled off on the shoulder to let the fire truck pass.

"Good. The firefighters from Palmetto are here." Shelley grabbed the door handle. "Stop the truck."

"What do you plan to do? Fight the fire with your bare hands? Leave it to the professionals."

She slapped the dash. "I need to do something. I can't just sit here and watch it burn."

"I'm going to keep driving so we can see how bad it is." Alan coughed from the smoke and pulled back onto the country road.

"No, the other way." She waved her hand. "I want to make sure Mom's house is still okay."

He gripped her hand as he drove, hard enough to squeeze the blood out of it.

"Do you think Starwood did this?" she asked.

"I know they did."

This was war. Not merely against the pack or Shelley, but him personally. They wouldn't have set the fire if he'd caved in to their demands and sold them the diner. *Not your problem*, a little voice told him. The Moonlight pack had a strong Alpha and plenty of capable men. They'd win the battle against the rival pack without him.

A vision of his brightly lit cubicle drifted through his mind as he drove in the dark. Was he really going to sit at his desk all day and do his job as if none of this had ever happened? Could he really bury the wolf in him again?

His fingertips dug into the steering wheel, a breath away from turning into claws. His rage against Starwood for destroying his mate's property made him want to shift so bad he ached. He wanted to howl and scream until his throat ripped to shreds.

For the first time in his life, he welcomed the beast

inside him. Even wanted to let it loose.

Maybe he should take Dad home with him so he could keep him safe. Shelley, too. But the way she perched in her seat and gripped the passenger door—as if she were about to leap through the open window—told him she'd never leave.

At last, he scooped cleaner air into his lungs, glad to see the flames hadn't touched the whole grove. Yet. Her ranch-style home appeared in the distance, unscathed.

She clasped her hands together under her chin. "Thank God the house is still okay."

"I'll drop you off so you can be with your mother," he said. "Meanwhile, I'm going to look for Starwood's goons, evidence, or both."

"No, I need to be involved." *With you.* Alan heard her unspoken words as clearly as the spoken ones.

She slid her cell phone out of her purse. "I'll call her again and let her know what's going on."

"I'm going to drive back to the blaze and see if the fire department found any evidence." He turned off onto one of the sandy dirt roads leading into the grove. "Be on the lookout for anything unusual like strange tire tracks."

"I wish it weren't so dark," she said with her head out the window as the truck bounced and squeaked over the ruts. "We'll need to look again in the morning. I mean, I will."

To hell she would. Before he could answer, she called her mother. The thought of her being alone in the orange grove tomorrow morning, or ever again, sent a bolt of lightning up his tailbone. His palms sweat, making the steering wheel slippery. What if the Starwood pack decided to take her hostage or kill her on the spot?

Obviously, she'd given up on begging him to stay. Well, she didn't have to convince him anymore. He couldn't leave. It was time to man up. Hadn't Dad been telling him that since he'd arrived?

Alan stopped the truck so suddenly the tires skidded in the sandy soil, sending them underneath a tree. An orange, ripe and perfect, dangled over the windshield.

"What is it?" Shelley jerked her head back inside the window and faced him. "Did you find anything?"

"No," he said, ripping open his fly. "I need to take care of something, and it can't wait."

Her eyes widened. "The bond? It's all right. We don't have to."

"Yes, we do." He shoved her wet shirt above her bare breasts. He swallowed. They were cool to the touch and as perfectly round as the fruit hanging over the truck. The nipples were already puckered from the wet fabric. His mouth watered to taste them, but he didn't have much time. He dragged his thumb across one, making her shudder.

"I'm sorry this is so rushed." He freed his erection from the damp work pants he wore. "Are you ready?"

To answer him, she knelt on the seat and pulled his hand to the cleft of her shorts. He groaned because the fabric was hot and wet from her juices. When he slid a finger inside, deep and hard, she writhed and groaned. Only she could make such practical clothes sexier than sin.

At least he'd made slow, tender love to her earlier. He should've done the bond then when he was more in control. Would it be safe to take her now with the beast in him so close to the surface?

He slid out from under the steering wheel. The simple movement clenched his balls. The searing smoke in his nostrils, mixed with the scent of her ripe pussy, was going to make him go off like a shot.

"Get on all fours and face the passenger window," he ordered. "You'd better hang onto it because I'm going to take you hard. I-I might lose control."

"I hope you do. Don't hold anything back."

Her words lit him up like the gasoline that had probably ignited the blaze. The sight of her bare, thrust-up derriere kindled another fire, this one in his groin. Between the two rounded globes lay her juicy center, slick and ready for him. Riper than any orange in the grove.

He pressed his hand sideways on top of her tailbone and lunged into her depths. The force of it stole his breath. Combined with the smoke, he choked and dropped forward. The movement set off a chain reaction in their bodies. His cock drove into her, high and upward like a hook. Her strangled cry tickled his ears, unchaining the beast inside him.

Her breaths whistled through clenched teeth while he pushed and thrust with unbelievable force. *Slow down. Be softer.* The warning voice yacking in his ear wouldn't shut up. The beast was loose, and he couldn't be anything but hard and rough. So hard the truck shook, shuddered, and rattled. He sunk his teeth into his bottom lip.

Please protect her from the beast because I am out of flipping control here.

Shelley's hot cream gushed around his cock. Her walls clamped down on him. Rippling like a roller coaster.

"Shit!" he bellowed as his own climax clenched his balls like a pit bull's jaws.

Growling, he grabbed a sheaf of her hair and exposed her neck. He shuddered when he ran his tongue across it, feeling her soft skin and tasting her orangey scent. His jaw went completely slack then closed like a vise, slow and strong. Her hips jumped under his, and she yelped when his teeth slid into her tender flesh. The coppery taste of her blood slid across his tongue.

So good. So right. Should have done it a long time ago.

After squeezing a last round of cum into her depths, his beast took over, blinding and deafening him. The truck lurched with enough force to tip over when he shifted. Fur struck his cheek. Shelley was shifting, too.

While their bodies jolted and transformed, he kept his teeth in her neck. If he let go, he'd lose her. Lose everything. She growled and whimpered. She bucked him off and leaped out the open window.

What the hell?

He leaped out after her. She tossed her head and loped away, a beautiful wolf with wheat-colored fur. He chased her as she raced between the trees like a slalom skier. Oranges dropped in the storm they left behind. With each yard she covered, she told him she wasn't easy. She was a challenge and a damn amazing one.

When he finally caught up with her, he lowered his head and aimed for a spot under her belly, knocking her off her feet. She rolled over, the fight gone out of her. She raised her feet, exposing her belly and her neck.

You're my mate, Alan.

Nuzzling the bloody fur at her neck, he licked until the wound he'd made sealed over. The wildness in him finally trickled out, and he shifted. In moments, he and Shelley lay naked in the sandy dirt, their arms locked around each other.

"I'm staying," he blurted out.

"Here in the grove?" she asked, blinking as if to clear dust from her eyes. "We should keep searching for clues, shouldn't we?"

He brushed back a damp lock of her hair. Her body was covered with a sheen of sweat like his. Under the moonlight, it looked delicious enough to taste.

"No, here in Moonlight." He started to add "after the crisis is over" but he wanted to stay longer, as in forever.

She squirmed out of his arms and sat up. "Don't feel obligated. I know how badly you want to go back."

"Not anymore." He smiled as he shook his head. "I *want* to be here, with you."

"Oh, Alan." She clasped both sides of his face and leaned her forehead against his. "You've made me the happiest wolf in Florida."

"I'm going to make sure you're also the safest wolf in Florida. I'd kill for you."

She brushed his cheek with her finger. "I know you would."

A shiver went through both of them. Would he be able to focus his rage on the enemy, or was the biggest threat to the Moonlight pack him? He hated to admit it, but the fire was a blessing. Without it, he would've been on that plane tomorrow like the coward he used to be.

After he grasped her hand, they stood. "Let's put some clothes on."

On their way back to the truck, she stopped short.

By instinct, he looped a protective arm around her back. "What's wrong? Did you see something?"

"No, I realized the prophecy I had of the pack needing you has come true."

It took a while to get back to the truck. Had they really run so far in wolf form?

After they dressed, Shelley bit her knuckle with a cry. "The sky is still glowing orange. What if the whole grove burns up?"

He started to say he wouldn't let that happen, but even his beast was no match against fire.

"I'm sure the fire department is doing everything it can," Alan said instead as he rubbed her shoulders. "Let's keep looking for clues."

He slid into the driver's seat and started the engine. Now that he was Shelley's true mate, would the pack finally accept him as one of their own?

***

The pack met in the diner at dawn. Shelley's eyes felt gritty and seared from smoke as she prepared the dining room for breakfast, laying out homemade jams and warm syrup. None of them had gotten any sleep last night. One-third of the grove had burned. A third! Even if insurance reimbursed her, she felt as if an equal proportion of her body had gone with it.

After breakfast, she planned to work the rest of the day in the grove, nursing damaged trees and harvesting any salvageable oranges from the dead ones. She wished she could shake the bad feeling— wrapping itself around her neck like smoke—she'd had all morning.

She stroked the scar there from Alan's teeth. Had he really made her his true mate? And was he really staying? Although she'd lost part of her farm, losing him would've been a hundred times worse. They could handle this, together.

The Palmetto County Sheriff's Department had found a gas can near where the blaze had started, proving it was arson, but not Starwood pack's involvement. While the Moonlight pack mainlined the coffee she'd brewed, they shared recent incidents of harassment.

Several members had received threats to sell their homes or they wouldn't have any left. An anonymous report had been made to the Manatee County Health Department that the diner might contain harmful bacteria.

"We need to beef up security," Derek said, attacking his steak and eggs. "Somebody grab some paper. We need to make a list of everything needing protection. I'll pass it on to our security agency, but we all need to keep our eyes open."

"We also need to send a couple of Defender guys into their territory to sniff around," Rand spoke up.

"Send Alan instead," Shelley suggested. "He's so upset about the fire he'll tear those wolves up."

"I thought he was leaving," Derek said.

"He's decided to stay." Pride for her mate lifted the fatigue from her shoulders.

Curtis made a sour face as he sipped some coffee. "He probably set it himself so he could look like a hero."

She clenched the empty jelly tray, restraining herself from knocking him over the head with it. Had she really once considered marrying such a bitter man? He was the reason Alan left the pack, and she wasn't about to let him change her mate's mind about staying.

"No, Curtis, that's something you would do."

As soon as the words came out of her mouth, she

regretted them. The pack needed to be united against its common enemy, not to have Curtis and Alan at each other's throats again.

"I'm glad he's sticking around," Derek said. "We need all the help we can get."

Approval of her mating bond from the Alpha sent a cleansing tide through her body, washing away the lingering smoke.

"If you get tired of farming, Shelley," Derek continued, "you might want to be a fortune teller because your prediction landed spot-on again."

"I could never compete with Riesa." Derek's human mate was a true psychic.

"When she's out of town, helping find missing persons like now, you can act as her backup."

"I'll try," Shelley promised. "I wish I'd been wrong this time, though."

She darted into the kitchen to deliver more orders the waitress had taken. Seeing Alan at the grill reminded her he planned to stay. He might even take over the diner. He thrust his cell phone into his pants pocket. When she handed him the order tickets, the sight of his worried face made her stomach sink. He hadn't changed his mind about staying, had he?

"What's wrong?" she asked. "Did you get a threatening call?"

"No, there's a crisis at my job. One of my programs in production is failing and the client is upset. My boss said if I didn't go back in the next day or two, I wouldn't have a job left. Getting a lousy reference from them wouldn't help me find another, either."

"I thought you were staying," she said in a small voice.

"I am."

"But knowing you could go back if you really

wanted to gave you a security blanket?" she suggested.

He nodded. "I'm sorry. It's not easy to switch lives so fast."

"I'll make it as smooth as possible." She pressed a kiss against his temple, the end of his bandana tickling her nose.

When Curtis flung open the kitchen door, Shelley instinctively took a step away from Alan. Even though he used to help out, he really had no reason to be in the kitchen now.

"What is it, Curtis?" she asked. "Were your grits too runny?"

"You two have performed the mating bond, haven't you?" he asked.

Shelley's cheeks flushed. "That's no business of—"

"We have," Alan said calmly. "Please return to the dining room. We're really busy here."

Instead, Curtis stalked closer. "You don't belong here, Scabs. Shelley's my woman, and I fucked her a hundred times before you ever got your cock into her."

Alan's spatula clattered across the grill. The beast was definitely awake. "Don't disrespect my woman that way. Apologize."

Instead, Curtis sneered and stepped closer. Desperation and pure hatred glowed in his blue eyes. Cold sweat broke out across Shelley's body. She backed against the wall, clutching an arm across her belly.

"It's all right," she said in the most soothing voice she could muster. "Curtis, I know you're upset, but resentment won't help. Please return to your seat."

"Was she good, Alan?" Curtis asked. "Did she moan when she looked at your messed-up face?

Climax when you sank those snaggly fangs into her neck? Or did she throw up on you?"

Shelley bit her knuckle, feeling helpless as she watched Alan's shoulders rise and fall with hard, ragged breaths. Several fangs popped out over his lips, slicing them, making them bleed.

"That's it," he bit out. After rummaging in the utensil drawer, he pulled out a long carving knife and knocked the whole metal cabinet over. It hit the tile floor with a deafening crash.

"Alan, don't!" she called out. "He's not worth it."

But he'd already thrown the knife at Curtis. It bounced off the metal door and ricocheted in tight, deadly spirals. Shelley watched, too frozen to move, as the long blade reflected the overhead lights.

And screamed as it stopped at last, slicing into her throat.

Chapter Nine

After Alan threw the knife, time froze. The hiss of oil on the grill, conversation from the dining room, and traffic from the nearby road vanished. Curtis and the order tickets dangling from the carousel vanished, too. He saw nothing but his mate—covered in blood. Waves of shock slammed into him. His muscles coiled in agony and vibrated with gut-deep tremors.

"Sh-Shelley." The words hurled into his throat, along with bile, but they made no sound.

"Holy shit!" Curtis floated in slow motion toward her. Bent down. "Oh, Shelley. Wake up, honey." Turned his head. Glared. "You goddamn freak! She's dead!"

When Alan's legs finally worked, he hobbled on them toward the wreckage. She couldn't be dead! Must be some mistake. Must be Dad. He was supposed to die soon, wasn't he? Not his beautiful mate. Strong. Healthy. In the prime of her life.

He fell when he reached her side. Dragged his nails across his scalp, hard enough to tear it. Bent down opposite Curtis. Touched her neck. Felt her blood slide through his fingers. Reminded him of his stinging lips. He touched them, too. Her blood mixed with his. They were one.

"Shelley." The word rasped out of him. "Oh my God. What have I done?"

She didn't answer. The blood on his fingers stained the white tank top he wore so it looked like hers. He had to lick her neck. Heal it over like he had the mating bond. He could heal her, couldn't he? He bent his head. Extended his tongue. Before he could reach her, someone pulled him away. He sniffed. Curtis. Angry Curtis.

Maybe the other man did this to her. Always jealous. Alan's head buzzed, and his stomach wavered from the sickening smell of blood. Too weak to fight him. Dragging him away.

The world sped up as the rest of the pack pushed in. Other men pulled him away, too. So far away he could barely see her anymore. He extended his hands until his arm sockets ached. Waved at the air like a restrained toddler. His heart hammered faster than a car with a stuck accelerator, but the beast in him stirred and fell. Even it was too broken to fight now.

"Fucking freak!" Curtis paced, his hands clenched in fists. "Look what he did to her!"

Women screamed. Men growled. The entire kitchen, a seething mass of motion like maggots in a carcass. Several gathered around Shelley. So pale. God, her lips so blue. Broken. Trying to fix her.

A wild-eyed Derek looked at her and then Alan. "Why would he do such a thing? They're mates."

"He's an unpredictable freak. That's why," Curtis snarled.

"Call the paramedics, please!" Barbara cried. "We can't fix her."

"No. We can't let outsiders know what we are," Derek exclaimed while Barbara pressed a wad of paper towels to Shelley's bleeding neck. "Where's our pack healer?"

"On vacation," Rand said.

"Effing great," Derek said. "Does anyone have needle and thread handy?"

"I have an emergency mending kit in my purse." Barbara's face paled. "D-do you want me to sew her up?"

"Yes," Derek said. "Brett, close the diner. I don't want any tourists to see this."

Not her, Alan wanted to growl. The conceited wolf wasn't Shelley's friend anymore, and he'd never liked the smell of her.

Liana took the paper towels from Barbara. "The bleeding has slowed."

"Good," Derek said. Then he gave orders to perform the impromptu surgery.

"Needs me," Alan cried. "Needs her mate."

"Over my dead body," Curtis said. "Lock him up before he kills someone else."

After grabbing a bottle of whiskey from the storeroom, Liana applied some to Shelley's neck. Barbara, looking as pale as Shelley, threaded her needle.

Alan stopped fighting and sagged in his restrainer's arms. "Let me hold her hand," he sobbed. "Please."

"Let him," Barbara said. "It can't hurt. Besides, I won't be able to concentrate with him bawling like that."

"All right," Derek agreed. "But keep him restrained."

As soon as the men dragged him toward her, he grasped her hand. So fragile. So cold. As if she'd already passed on.

Please don't die. Please don't die.

Clammy nausea pressed around him as he watched the needle weave in and out of Shelley's flesh. The same spot where he'd given her the mating bite last night. Her moans of ecstasy in the truck haunted him. So beautiful in her dress at their candlelight dinner. The softness in her hazel eyes when she told him she loved him. Memories tumbled through his mind in pieces with no logic or order.

Logic. He may never be able to program software again. To think he sweated losing his boring job. Nothing mattered but her. He caressed her fingers, testing the length of each bone between his thumb and forefinger. Her skin felt soft but tough from the hard work she did.

Why hadn't he flown home this morning as he'd originally planned? He knew a beast lived inside him—a dangerous weapon that could detonate at any time. The moon shone past half-full now, too. In Florida, his beast seemed to stay active through the whole damn lunar cycle. He'd stayed to protect Shelley from Starwood, but Curtis was right. He presented a much bigger danger to her than anything they could do.

If only he could erase everything, beginning with his trip down here. He could have talked to Dad on the phone or through videoconferencing. She'd always been too good for him. He'd been delusional to think she could ever be his.

He had to get back to northern Virginia before he hurt someone else.

"Almost done," Barbara said.

Shelley's fast, shallow breaths slowed and evened out. Alan's heartbeat finally slowed, too, clearing his mind. Luckily, she slept. He couldn't handle seeing the accusation in her eyes yet.

The kitchen door burst open, and Eileen, Shelley's mother, rushed in. Her face and knees crumpled at the sight of her daughter on the floor in a pool of blood. Alan avoided her gaze, sure she'd treat him like Curtis when she found out what he'd done.

"My baby!" she shrieked, pulling at her hair, which was darker and shorter than her daughter's. "Oh God. What happened?"

Derek gripped both her arms, preventing her from falling. "We're going to get to the bottom of it once she's stabilized."

"All done," Barbara said, tying off the thread and cutting it. When Liana handed her a bandage, she placed it over the wound.

"Let's get her home, so she can rest," Eileen said.

Derek sent two men to load her into the woman's car and see them safely to her home. Letting go of her hand was the hardest thing Alan had ever done. What if she died? What if he couldn't be with her when she took her last breath?

"Good job, Barbara," Derek said, squeezing her shoulders as she mopped up the blood. "I nominate you as the pack's backup healer."

"Thanks." When she looked up from wringing a bloody rag into the nearby bucket, her face was green. "I'm not so sure, though. I think I'm gonna be sick."

"Me, too," Liana said. "First the fire and now this."

Derek inclined his head toward the door. "Dining room. Pack meeting."

Alan's stomach sank. The time for pack justice had arrived. He squared his shoulders as two men led him out like a prisoner and sat him at one of the tables. Whatever his punishment would be, he'd take it like a man.

"Should we tie him up?" one asked Derek.

"Not necessary," Alan said.

Derek and Curtis sat with him at the round table. The other pack members sat nearby.

"All right," Derek said. "What happened. Curtis, you first."

"Isn't it clear?" The wolf shot Alan a scowl. "He got pissed off and threw a knife at Shelley."

Curtis's nasty words leading up to the attack had cut Alan deeper than any knife could have, but admitting it would make him sound like a baby.

"I don't believe he'd throw a knife at his mate," Derek said. "What or who pissed him off?"

Curtis tossed his head. "We exchanged a few words. Everyone was pretty uptight after the fire."

"Did he throw the knife at you?" the Alpha asked.

"How should I know?" His shoulders twitched, as if chasing off a fly. "It flew so fast."

"Did you duck?" Derek jabbed a finger into the man's breastbone. "So help me, Curtis, if you don't tell the truth, I'm going to punish you, too."

"Can't remember. I might have."

Coward. Alan would have jumped in front of her to save her life. He would die for her. Curtis's gut reaction to save his own hide didn't surprise him.

Derek looked to Alan next. "Your turn. What happened?"

"I was exhausted from the fire and trying to get out the breakfast orders. Curtis walked in and gave me a bunch of crap about mating with Shelley. I lost control and threw the knife at him. He ducked, and it ricocheted off the door, hitting her."

"I believe you," Derek said. "Sounds like an unfortunate accident."

"Accident, my ass! That crazy nut tried to kill me."

Curtis pounded the table with his fist. "Throw him out of the pack right now. If you don't, I will."

Other voices in the room supported his suggestion, but Derek growled a warning. "I'll give the orders around here."

Alan raised his hand. "No need. I canceled today's flight, but I'll be out of here as soon as I can book another one."

"Don't go yet." The Alpha appraised him with narrowed eyes. "Shelley predicted we'll need you against the Starwood threat. When she recovers, I'll let her decide your fate."

"Say what?" Curtis argued.

Derek eyed Alan and Curtis. "And you're both ordered to stay away from each other."

On numb legs, Alan hobbled out to his car. Nothing to do now but wait at his father's house for Shelley's verdict. He wished Dad hadn't lived to see his son become the world's biggest failure.

Hopefully, she'd dream up the worst punishment imaginable. Probably deserved to have his balls cut off for threatening her life. He hoped she'd decide soon.

If she lived.

***

The next morning, Shelley lay in her bed, still weak from the loss of blood. A handmade quilt with motifs of orange fruits, leaves, and blossoms covered her. When she'd woken up, she hadn't remembered anything except the grove fire. How had her neck gotten cut?

Mom had served her breakfast on a tray and told her everything, including Alan's involvement. As her strength returned, so did her own memories—the angry words, the knife flying through the air.

Oh, Alan. Why? Couldn't you have stopped yourself?

Her concern had less to do with her injury than fear of what the pack would do to him. He'd kept telling her he was dangerous and couldn't be trusted, but she'd always refused to believe it.

Her mother had told her Curtis and several others were on a witch hunt. Thank goodness Derek had a level head.

"They're here," Mom said, poking her head in her bedroom door.

"I want to see Alan alone," Shelley replied.

"Are you sure that's wise, honey?"

"I insist."

A few minutes later, the door opened and Alan drifted in as gently as a wisp of smoke. His shoulders and head were so hunched he looked half his normal size. She could hardly believe he was the same person as the enraged man who'd thrown the knife. Tears flowed down her cheeks. Last night during the mating bond, they'd had it all. Love. A beautiful future. Her dreams were gone now. They'd leaked out on the diner floor with her blood.

"Come closer, Alan," she said, extending her arm. "Look at me."

He stepped to the side of the bed and sat on the edge of it. When he finally looked at her, his cheeks were stained with tears, too.

"God, Shelley. I'm so sorry." He lifted her hand, kissed it, and pressed it to his cheek. His tears, warm as blood, flowed across her skin.

"Don't cry. It was an accident," she said, clearing her throat to steady her voice. "And I'm feeling stronger. I'm going to live."

"I'm so thankful." He laid her hand gently on the quilt. "Derek wants you to decide my fate. Don't hold back."

"Curtis caused the incident," she said. "I can't punish you. I love you."

"Don't love me." He turned his head as his shoulders shook with a silent sob. "Whatever you do, don't love me. I don't deserve it."

"I can't help it. You're my mate, and I believe the good in you." She caressed his wet cheek. "I'm not giving up on you, damn it!"

"You'd change your mind if the beast in me actually killed somebody. But I'm not going to stay and let that happen. I was a fool to even try."

She threaded her fingers through his. "Listen to me, Alan. Lying here has given me a lot of time to think."

"Yeah?" His chocolate-brown eyes, wary and dark with pain, looked at her.

"First, it drove me crazy to lie still." She plucked at her nightgown. "I realized I work too hard."

"You do." He stroked her thumb. "You're always taking care of everybody else. It's your turn to be taken care of."

She gazed out the window. "I guess I never forgave myself for what happened on prom night."

He squeezed her fingers. "What happened then was my fault, not yours."

"The second thing I realized is love can heal you, Alan," she said, gazing at him again.

"I doubt it." He shook his head so hard, the ends of his bandana flapped.

"I came up with a theory."

His full lips curved into a tender smile, but his

eyes were wary. She refused to let his skepticism dampen the excitement beating in her chest.

"Get Derek up here. I want him to hear this, too."

When he left to get the Alpha, she gripped the quilt. They had to believe her. She wasn't about to let go of her true mate, and the fire last night proved the pack needed him more than ever.

The men entered. Derek sat on a Windsor chair in the corner while Alan resumed his seat on her bed.

"You would never intentionally harm me or your father, would you?" she asked her man. "Even if you lost complete control."

He shrugged. "I'd like to think not, but who knows? When I lose control, I lose it."

"You can't hurt us because we're part of your pack. I'm your mate, and Don is your father."

"The pack hates me."

"When I say pack, I don't mean Moonlight. You've never been part of it, or the old one, because they've always rejected you."

Derek looked down but didn't argue with her.

"What can I do for you?" Alan smoothed her quilt. "Do you need anything? Magazines? Tea?"

She grabbed his arm. "Listen to me. This is important."

"The only thing I can do is go back north where this shit doesn't get triggered." He jumped off the bed and paced.

"What I'm trying to say...." Still weak, she paused to catch her breath. "Is if Moonlight pack fully embraced you, you'd be no danger to it."

"I'm not going to risk staying around long enough to find out."

"You have to," she insisted. "If not for me, for the pack."

He shook his head. With downcast eyes, he kissed her forehead. The brush of his bandana on her skin reminded her of the other times they'd kissed. She'd rather slit her throat back open than lose him.

"Take care, Shelley," he murmured. "I'll always love you, wherever I am."

After a last squeeze of her hand, he walked toward the door. If he walked through it, she'd never see him again. She had to try her experiment. If it succeeded, he might stay, but if it failed, Derek might do worse to him than exile him from the pack. She might even endanger herself again.

The hardest risk of all was losing his love. Watching it turn to hate. But, she had to do it for him and the pack. She believed so strongly in love, she decided to try.

"Coward," she said in the snarliest voice she could muster. "Go ahead and walk out."

He turned his head, his eyes filled with hurt. His mouth opened, as if he were going to say something.

She bit down on a knuckle. "I always liked Curtis better, anyway. He has a bigger dick."

Rage, pain, and confusion flashed through his eyes. Instead of opening the door, he flung it open. Good. Her ploy was working. Her limbs trembled beneath the quilt because hurting him felt worse than the knife slicing into her neck.

Derek stood. "Shelley, I don't think it's a good idea to taunt him."

"What's the matter, Scabs?" she asked, ignoring her Alpha. "Getting hot under the collar? Why don't you finish me off, you miserable freak?"

"Why are you...acting...like Curtis?" he bit out. "I thought you loved me."

His shoulders heaved, and he gripped the

doorframe, looking as if he were about to shred the boards to splinters with his bare hands. Fear gnawed her spine. What if her theory was wrong? What if he lost control and lunged at her? Derek would surely kill him on the spot. No, she'd gone this far. She had to see it through.

Now, for the final thrust.

"Don't tell me you believed when me I said I really wanted you in high school." She even tossed her hair, reliving the arrogant beauty queen she'd once been. "I played a joke on you on prom night, and I've been playing you ever since you got here."

She gripped the quilt until her knuckles turned white. Alan roared, letting out a primal howl so pain ridden it stood the hairs on her neck on end. Her breath froze in her lungs as she watched him. Even Derek's eyes looked twice their normal size. If her mate was going to attack her, he'd do it now. He froze, too, breathing hard as fangs popped through his lips.

The door banged behind him as he ran from the room. Shaking, Shelley closed her eyes and let out the breath she'd been holding. He'd passed the test.

Derek raced to the window after the front door slammed, shaking the house. "You might have asked my permission before trying something so dangerous."

"The point is he didn't hurt me. The pack must fully accept him. Then we'll never have to fear him." She held out her hands to him. "Aren't I always right?"

He nodded. "Yes, but if you're wrong about this, he could hurt someone else."

"Then I take full responsibility," she said. "Talk to the others, especially Curtis. If I can't live with my mate, I'm not sure I want to live at all."

"Don't say that." Derek stepped closer and squeezed her foot through the quilt. "You're one of our most valuable members."

"I mean it," she shot back. "And after last night's fire, the Starwood pack is an even bigger threat than I first thought. We need his fighting skills."

Derek slipped his hands into his pockets. "We have plenty of strong men."

"Ones that will fight to the death without thinking?"

Realizing she had to convince him more than Alan, Shelley ripped off her bandage and smeared her finger through the healing wound. "What is this?"

He winced. "Blood."

"Blood comes from violence, enemy against enemy," she blurted out. "It also stands for kinship. One pack, one blood."

He nodded but didn't speak.

"Alan would be Moonlight's most loyal pack member, but only if you accept him. Against any enemy outside the pack, he'd be a killing machine. The best weapon you've got."

Before he could answer her, his cell phone rang. After he answered it, anguish swept across his features. "Who is this?"

She crossed her fingers. *Please don't let Alan be injured or in deeper trouble.*

"Is Alan all right?" she asked after he pocketed the phone.

"That was an anonymous caller. He said if we don't evacuate our homes and businesses, they'll be destroyed."

"Oh, no. Starwood, again. What should we do?"

"You and your mother need to stay in the house."

He bit his lip and loped from the room.

Her heart and Alan's fate—as well as the pack's—were in his hands now. She had done everything she could.

Chapter Ten

By the time Alan arrived at his father's place, he'd sweat so much his clothes felt painted on. It was a wonder he'd arrived in one piece. His eyes had been so blurry and wet he'd barely seen the road. His hands weren't too steady on the wheel, either.

Yeah, hell, he'd cried like an effing baby. Because he'd believed in Shelley's love and couldn't stand to be the pack's prize fool once again. He was old enough to know better.

He closed the front door behind him and staggered against it. The beast coiled at the base of his spine and filled his lungs with silent howls. He held his trembling hands, palms up, and stared at them. His beast had popped out so often down here, he was almost used to it.

His body ached to do something—usually, to tear someone's head off. When he'd thrown the knife in the diner, he'd wanted to slit Curtis's throat open. Not Shelley's. How could she have acted so cruel to him? Had she really made a fool of him all along? Every time she'd gazed at him with tender passion, had she been laughing at him inside?

His fingers convulsed. Did he want to tear her

apart? No, he couldn't picture it, even if he tried. If Curtis had been the one lying in bed, tossing insults at him, he would have jumped on him and tried to strangle him.

Not Shelley. He hadn't even touched her. She was his mate. He couldn't hurt his father, either. No matter how out of control the beast made him, it seemed to be programmed not to harm the ones he loved.

Maybe her theory was right, after all. He tugged off his sweaty bandana and let out a shaky breath followed by a laugh. Her theory. Yeah.... She'd tested him. The love she'd shown him over the past few days couldn't be faked, but a tiny part of him wasn't sure. How could someone so beautiful and giving want an ugly, violent freak like him?

He stared at the bandana, which he only wore here in Florida. Even though he knew he'd never harm her intentionally, being caught in the crossfire of his rage had almost killed her. He couldn't take that chance again.

The aroma of country ham drew him to the kitchen. Although he wasn't hungry, the wolf in him craved meat to replace the energy he'd spent. Rita stood in front of the stove, and his father sat at the table.

Rita turned. "Good morning, Alan. I'll fix you a plate."

"Thanks," he replied, taking a seat at the table.

"How's Shelley?" Dad asked.

"Recovering," Alan said.

"Don't blame yourself." To his surprise, his father's frail hand covered his. "Curtis is a first-class ass."

Alan grabbed a piece of ham from the plate Rita

gave him and swallowed after a couple of bites. "Move north with me."

Dad dropped his fork. "Why the hell would I want to do that?"

"This place is bad for me." He glared at the charred orange grove out the window. "I want Shelley to come, too. We can even open another restaurant if you want."

"I'm dying. I don't have the energy to open a lemonade stand, let alone another restaurant."

Alan rubbed his forehead. "I thought you wanted me to change my career to the restaurant business."

"Unless you plan to run Moonlight Diner, I don't give a rat's ass what you do." He released a wheezy sigh. "This is my home now. I want to die here."

Alan stared at his plate and nodded. Shelley would probably feel the same way. Maybe they would change their minds and follow him after he left. A chill made him shudder, jiggling the silverware at his plate.

For the first time, the thought of being alone scared him worse than the beast.

Rita placed a stack of pancakes on the table. "I'll come back to clean up when you're done."

"You're never going to stop feeling sorry for yourself, are you?" the old man asked, eating a pancake with his fingers.

"How can I?" Alan ripped his pancake in half and dragged it through a puddle of syrup. "This fucked-up wolf almost killed his mate. At least give me the dignity of leaving before the pack throws me out."

"I hate to break it to you, but nobody's perfect. Isn't being born and enjoying life worth the flaws we have to put up with?"

"For most people and wolves," Alan replied. "Not

me."

"Well, you're not that damn special," Don groused. "It's high time you got over yourself and made the best of things."

Alan left his breakfast half-eaten on his plate, and bolted toward the phone. He had the number for the airline memorized. Closing his eyes, he imagined himself suspended in the sky, getting away from this place. He'd deal with the loneliness. It had to be better than this gut-wrenching misery of not belonging.

As soon as he touched the phone, it rang. The vibration raced up his arm, making the beast in him jump.

"Alan?" As soon as he heard Shelley's voice, he wished he hadn't answered it.

"I didn't mean any of it!" she cried. "I was testing you."

"I know." He whispered the words so softly, he wasn't sure if she heard them.

"I'm so sorry." The emotion in her voice reached through the phone and caressed him like a gentle hand. "You know I love you."

When tears leaked from his eyes and raced down his cheeks, he batted them away. "It doesn't change anything."

"Of course it does," she protested. "It was the only way to prove *your* pack is immune to the anger."

"But you weren't immune. You still got caught in the crossfire." He paced. Dishes clinked in the kitchen as Rita cleaned up. "I'm too violent, and it won't change as long as I'm here."

"It's a violent world, Alan. Look at what a rival pack did to us three years ago."

"I'm not a rival pack. I'm supposed to be safe." He

let out a raspy sigh. "Come north with me, Shelley. We could build a new life."

The silence on the other end lasted so long, he wondered if she'd not heard him or if the line had gone dead. Memories of holding her drifted through his mind, her orange-sweet scent so intense he almost smelled it. Would they fade as the years without her passed by?

"Shelley? Please say yes. Dad refuses, but I could take him along for his own good."

"Don't do this," she answered with a sob in her voice. "Don't make me choose."

"Virginia has farmland, too. We could live in the country and have an apple orchard. The winter nights are colder, but I'd keep you warm."

She sniffed. "You know I can't leave the pack."

"I'm leaving." Alan squeezed the phone while a new layer of sweat covered his head. "With or without you."

"Wait," she called out before he could hang up. "The Starwood pack called Derek after you left. They said if we don't evacuate our homes and businesses, they'll be destroyed."

"Then you have to come with me. Have your mother pack you a bag. She can come, too."

"No, you have to stay and fight. The pack needs you!"

He gripped his forehead. "What the pack needs is to get rid of internal threats like me. It needs to focus on the external enemy."

"Then don't come over. Just go." She hung up, the dial tone sounding like the flat line of a once-beating heart.

***

Two days later, the Moonlight pack gathered at Citrus Lake. Shelley swiped back a hank of hair as she helped set food on the outdoor tables. With Alan's help, The Defenders had taken out Starwood's Alpha and second-in-command yesterday in a raid.

Pack members threw tonight's party to celebrate a new era of peace and to wish Alan farewell. His flight left tomorrow. With swimming in mind, she'd worn a pink bikini under her shorts.

Nothing mattered more than the pack's safety, she kept reminding herself as she lit the centerpiece candles and set out beer glasses. She'd barely slept last night, wondering what it would be like to go north with him and live the life of a human.

She couldn't leave the pack if she wanted to. It was part of her. Without it to care for, she'd be dead inside. It would kill their love. And if it didn't kill her spirit, it would eventually sicken her and kill her body. Of course, being without her mate might do the same thing.

After she lit another candle, she coaxed the tiny flame along with the hope struggling to take root inside her. Tonight's farewell included a ceremony to officially claim Alan as part of the Moonlight pack. If he felt the sincerity deeply enough, maybe he would stay.

When Derek left the barbecue hog spit, he caught her eye and nodded. The ceremony was on. Alan pulled up in his rental car. He and Rita helped his father out. The older man wore a short-sleeved shirt with a bright tropical print Shelley hadn't seen him wear in years. She led them to a table while country rock played in the background.

"Something smells damn good," Don said. "I could

eat a horse."

"We have a whole pig on the spit," Rand replied, "but we've got something planned first."

Shelley squeezed Alan's lean waist and gave the end of his black bandana a playful tug. In his matching black tank top and jeans, he looked like a sexier-than-sin bandit. How could she ever let him go?

He kissed her on the cheek. "What's going on?"

Derek motioned him to the center table and handed him an unlit candle. "Hold this."

"Why?" he asked.

"I'm inducting you into the Moonlight pack." Derek picked up a lit candle and held it in front of him.

"Are you sure?" Alan asked. "I was never really part of the old pack."

"That's been the problem the whole time," the Alpha said.

"What is this?" Alan narrowed his eyes at Curtis, who stood with crossed arms but a neutral expression on his face. "Another joke? Can't you people let me leave with a little dignity? I promise I'll never bother you again."

Shelley clasped her hands together as Alan plopped the unlit candle on the table and headed toward the car.

"Eat up, Dad," he muttered. "Rita, bring him to the car when he's ready to go home."

"No, no, no," Barbara said, darting from the crowd to grab his arm. "The guest of honor is not allowed to leave the party."

Pinching her lips together to keep them from quivering, Shelley stepped in front of him.

"I can't stop you from leaving, Alan, but let the

pack do this for you. Please. I swear it's not a trick."

A heavy sigh shook his shoulders, but he headed back to the table and picked up the unlit candle.

"Do you accept this pack as yours, wherever you are, and me as your Alpha?" Derek asked.

When Alan's dark gaze—vulnerable and questioning—sought Shelley's face, she smiled at him with all the love she felt in her heart.

"I do," he said hoarsely.

Derek lit his candle and picked up a small knife. Everyone watched as the Alpha ran the blade across his forearm, leaving behind a red line. Moonlight glistened on the drops of blood. When he handed Alan the knife, the other man hesitated a moment. Shelley bit her lip, tasting her own blood.

Finally, he rolled up his sleeve and sliced—ever so slowly—his own arm. After turning it face up, he held it toward Derek.

The other man covered the wound with his. "We are one pack, one blood. Curtis?"

Shelley held her breath as everyone stared at Alan's rival with expectant eyes. What was going on? The pack bonding ceremony usually occurred between a wolf and its Alpha.

After standing still for several long seconds, he finally walked over and took the knife from Alan.

"Well, this won't be the first scar I've borne for you." With a grunt, he cut his flesh.

The sight of his blood reminded her of prom night, making her stomach rebel against the party food she'd snacked on earlier. Alan stared at it, too, his lips twitching. Would it incite the beast in him? If Derek had discussed this part of the ceremony with her, she would have talked him out of it. It was too dangerous.

To her surprise, the men rubbed their arms

together, smearing their mingled blood. One pack. One blood.

"We're brothers now," Curtis declared.

Shelley rushed forward to wipe their wounds with a wet cloth Barbara supplied. Because the other woman had saved her life and helped plan tonight's ceremony, their friendship was stronger than ever.

"Oh, Curtis. Alan." She wiped tears with the back of her arm. "I'm so amazed. So proud."

"Let's get the party started," Curtis said. "I'm going to snag some pork before your father eats it all."

Shelley slid her arms around Alan and squeezed. "Thank you. That was the most beautiful thing I've ever seen."

"I'm still leaving," he said.

Her heart fell to her knees. "I know. Eat quickly. I want to do some things to you underwater."

And a lot more after that. He might be leaving, but she planned to make love to him until the moment his plane left the ground.

He smiled against her temple. "Promise?"

Under the moon, the Moonlight pack danced to southern blues and rock. They tore into the roast pig, leaving nothing but a carcass, and washed it down with cold beer. Before long, splashes filled the air as they flung off their clothes and raced into the warm, dark lake water.

She only ate a few bites of food because she wanted Alan more. They clung to a thicket of reeds at the side of the pond. He slipped his hand down the back of her wet bathing suit. Loving the possessive way he caressed her buttocks, she looped her arm around his wet shoulders.

When he eased a finger into her depths, her head

dropped back. The moonlight flooded her eyes as his lips grazed hers. His breath and beard tickled and teased, igniting a fire brighter than the one that had claimed part of her orchard.

Her mate. Her man. If only for tonight.

He slid another finger inside her, expanding and tightening her core at the same time.

"I need you," she muttered. "All of you."

"Here in public?"

"Who cares?" she laughed. "We're all family now."

The surface of the water between them ruffled as he fumbled with himself below. In seconds, the hot, smooth head of his cock entered her folds. Not stopping. Not asking. Taking. Her knees drifted toward the surface while each muscle in her body went slack. Every nerve centered on the spot where they joined. She would have slipped below and drowned if his unique energy didn't fill her body, making her feel so hot and full.

"Alan," she said, followed by a sigh. Forming a tight seal around his flesh, she felt every ridge and vein. Would never forget...how he felt. How he sounded when a growl of pleasure vibrated his throat. He may have bonded with the other men in blood, but this was how they joined.

Grasping her hips, he held her immobile and helpless to resist his pounding thrusts. As if she wanted to. His mouth tasted so delicious, better than any barbecue. Her tongue went wild, exploring every inch of his full lips. He sucked it deep into his mouth while he seated himself even deeper in her womb.

He couldn't leave! It wasn't physically possible when they were so close.

Hopefully, no one suspected what they were doing. Not that she cared. He was her man, and she'd never felt more primitive. More like a wolf. For the first time in years, she didn't give a damn about farming or taking care of others. The last thing she wanted was to be a shallow, self-centered teenager again. She simply wanted to fill her needs, and what she needed was him. His cock, his love, his presence.

She locked her legs around him and rode him hard. Taking, taking, taking. Her fingers, as frantic as her swollen cleft ringing his cock, roved over his scalp, memorizing every curve.

Mmm.... Maybe she could visit him often. The pack didn't need her here every minute of every day, did it?

Each nerve in her clitoris pulsed, so raw and sensitive it nearly drove her out of her mind. Her hair, damp from the water and their sweat, slapped against her neck. As they moved, her hard, achy nipples rubbed against his hot, wet chest. Nothing had ever felt more perfect. More right.

A sharp yip escaped her throat when her pelvis exploded. She mashed her chest against his. Dug her nails into his shoulders to keep from drowning. His teeth scraped across her neck and closed around a tendon, mimicking the mating bite he'd once etched there. The teasing sensation made her buck even harder, hammering herself onto his cock. When his hot seed bathed her, she gasped and gazed up at the moon.

It was three-quarters full—close enough to her fertile time to be risky.

He grasped her chin, possessively like a true mate. "What's wrong?"

"Nothing." If she couldn't have him, she might have his child, but she wouldn't tell him so to keep him here. The new pack could use some pups. How she would love to have the first.

He let out a breath. "That was incredible."

"It just gets better and better." Or it could, if he stayed.

When the rest of the lake finally came into focus, she realized the party was still going on without them. But something drew her eyes to the road where several of the pack's vehicles were parked. As if he sensed her sudden unease, Alan glanced in the same direction.

Two motorcycles pulled up. Tall, burly men dressed in black leather got off and stalked toward the party. More bikes arrived—a hornet's nest of throbbing engines that drowned out the music—and parked farther away.

"I-it's the Starwood pack," she said, gasping. "What's left of it. They must be here for revenge."

"Holy orange pulp! They've got guns." He squeezed her hand underwater. "Stay here. Duck and hold your breath if you have to. Promise?"

She nodded as her heart flopped in her chest like a hooked fish. *Don't let him die,* she thought, wishing he'd left before now so he'd be safe. She didn't want any of them to die. Her entire pack was here. Starwood must have heard about the party and known their defenses would be down.

Heaven help them all.

Chapter Eleven

Shelley clung to the reeds at the side of the lake. The male wolves of Moonlight pack shifted and circled the invaders. The guns in their hands made it clear they hadn't come to talk. Her heart beat so fast she could barely breathe. The urge to shift yanked her muscles and ached in her bones, but she could navigate water better in human form.

Her focus attached to Alan. First, he pulled his father and Rita to the ground. Huddling, they shivered under the table. Luckily, the marauders fixed their attention on someone else. One of them aimed at his belly and tried to bowl him over.

Shelley blinked, unable to believe the festive barbecue had turned into a battlefield. Music still played in the background. The pig carcass, gruesome looking in the shadows, still smoked.

Shots fired and Brett went down. He writhed in agony, paws in the air. The sight of blood spilling on the ground pulled her into a shift she couldn't control. Her pack needed her.

She jumped out of the water and stuck to the perimeter of the fighting. When one of the rival wolves went after Curtis, aiming for his jugular, a million thoughts flew through her mind. She remembered their relationship, imperfect but a comfort over the years without Alan.

A hair-raising howl filled the air, and the entire atmosphere seemed to explode as Alan jumped off one of the tables. At the same moment, one of the thugs aimed a gun at his chest, but he didn't look, as if he saw no one but Curtis.

With a feral growl, he locked his jaws into the throat of Curtis's attacker, bringing him down. And he didn't stop there. Whipping his head from side to side, he tore out pieces of flesh. A pale windpipe, severed and bloody, dangled from the ripped patch of fur.

As soon as the attacker's jaws released, Curtis rolled under a table. A flash filled the air as a shot fired. Alan lunged away, but not quite far enough. A red hole bloomed in his hindquarters as he sailed through the air.

A squeaky grunt spilled from his throat when his legs hit the ground, but he didn't stop. Shelley dodged here and there with her belly low to the ground. She couldn't keep her eyes off her mate. As soon as it was safe, she needed to tend to him.

To her surprise, he didn't stop. With his back left leg practically dangling in its socket, he lunged toward the man with the gun, knocking him down with both forepaws. The gun fired once more, safely into the air this time.

Alan's jaws worked again, making hamburger of that throat, too. She'd never seen such a vicious killing machine in her life. Prom night had been a tea party compared to this. She yelped when a club descended on his skull. That didn't stop him, either.

Bloody spittle clung to his sharp, crooked fangs in

long strings. The wild expression in his brown eyes asked, *Who's next?* Her heart battered her ribcage. What if he turned on their pack as well? What if he was so out of control he didn't know the difference? Her theory about kinship was about to be put to the biggest test yet.

He didn't harm any Moonlight members. His heroics gave the rest of their pack an advantage. Soon, the invaders were surrounded and started retreating to their motorcycles, leaving several dead behind.

When they were finally gone, Shelley shifted to human so she could tend to the injured more easily.

"Oh my God!" Barbara cried, her jeans practically ripped to shreds. "If I'd known this would happen, I would have brought more needle and thread."

Shelley raced to her mate's side. He'd resumed human form again, too, gasping and gripping his bloody thigh. The rest of him bled so much she couldn't tell where one wound began and the other ended.

"Don't you dare die on me," she cried, raining kisses above his cut lips.

He gazed up at her with chocolate-brown eyes. "It's going to take a lot more than that to kill me."

She'd never forget those eyes—hard and opaque when he fixed them on his enemies, but warm and melted for her.

Curtis shifted to human form and gripped his hand. "Y-you saved my life. Thank you."

"Of course I did," Alan said. "We're brothers."

Shelley used a wadded-up napkin to help block the flow of blood from his thigh. Derek limped over, as patched and bloody as many others.

"You were amazing, Alan," he said, squeezing his

arm. "The best weapon we've got."

"Hear, hear," Rand seconded, holding up a fresh beer.

"My theory about kinship was right," Shelley pointed out. "I'm always right, Derek. Remember that."

He laughed. "I will. Tonight proved why each species has mutations. What might not fit into everyday life is exactly what's needed in times of crisis."

"All my life I've been trying to fight my instinct with logic." Alan blinked at the moon. "I never dreamed being a freak could be a good thing."

"It's a really good thing," Derek agreed, "but I wish we could avoid the violence between packs. We're like gangs. We took down their leaders, so they came here for revenge."

"Maybe integrating with other packs should be an option," Shelley suggested.

"Peace sounds good to me, too." Alan winced. "Bullets hurt."

Derek gripped his shoulder. "As your Alpha, I'm ordering you to stay and rest for a few days before you fly home."

Alan gazed into Shelley's eyes. "I am home." Then he raised himself up to his elbows and looked around. "Where's Dad?"

She pushed him back down. "Rita walked him to the car. They're safe."

Thanks to her amazing mate, they all were and would be for a very long time.

Epilogue

Two weeks later, Alan parked in the Moonlight Diner parking lot. The sky was dark, but lights and music from his diner spilled outside. Yes, his. He'd turned in his rental car and bought a used pickup truck. He wouldn't earn as much money slinging hash as he did as a computer programmer, but he had all the riches he needed here. Home.

Near the front door, a woman in a pink satin dress smiled at him. Her silky blonde hair had never looked more smooth and perfect.

Feeling like a high-school kid again, Alan stopped before her and cleared his throat. Then he pulled a heavy square of paper from the pocket of the black dress slacks he wore. What if she played the same joke on him? Impossible. Too much had happened.

"I received this invitation." He held it out to her. "Did you send it?"

"I did," she replied, love gleaming in her hazel eyes.

"Then these are for you." He handed her a bouquet filled with orange blossoms.

Rita had helped him with it. Dad had even sprayed him down with enough cologne to kill a skunk.

Everyone seemed determined to give him the perfect evening.

Shelley buried her nose in the flowers, inhaled, and sighed. His pants tightened below the belt. He'd never get tired of hearing her earthy sounds of pleasure.

"Shall we?" she asked, opening the door.

When they stepped inside, the lights dimmed. The tables were pushed near the walls and covered with white tablecloths and sparkly centerpieces. Streamers hung suspended from the ceiling fans. Some of the pack members, musical instruments in hand, stood on a makeshift stage near the kitchen door. The rest of them, dressed in formal attire, sat at the tables.

She drew him to the center of the room, placed one of his hands on her waist, and clasped his other one. The band launched into a romantic song popular in their high-school days. He'd come a long way from being the class freak.

"May I have this dance?" she asked.

"You may, and a whole lot more." He pressed his palm into the small of her back, showing the world she was his.

Their bodies clung together, rotating across the floor. He inhaled her orange scent, her beauty, and her love. New memories painted over the painful ones from high school.

She ran her fingers across his bare scalp, sending delicious shivers down his legs. "No bandana tonight?"

"Not tonight," he said, grinning at her. "Didn't seem dressy enough."

"Darn. I was looking forward to taking it off."

He ran his lips across her earlobe, nipping and teasing. "I have plenty of other things you can take off later."

"Promise?"

"Seriously, though. Thank you for this. I don't know what to say."

"Say you'll stay," she whispered. "Forever."

He pressed a kiss to her mouth. "I took over the diner, didn't I?"

"I know, but part of me is afraid something will happen and you'll leave again."

"Nothing is going to happen, Shelley," he said, leaning his forehead against hers. "The next time we dance will be at our wedding."

She stopped dancing. "I-is that a proposal?"

"You're the psychic," he said, flashing a grin at her. "You tell me."

"Yes, Alan." Her eyes glowed with unshed tears. "Yes, I'll marry you."

Everyone clapped, which sounded better to him than the music. He held her closer, pulling them back into the slow, romantic beat.

"I expect my wife to hand feed me an orange every day," he said.

"I thought you hated oranges."

"I don't hate anything anymore," he said quietly. "And I love oranges now. Almost as much as I love you."

About the Author

Afton Locke is a USA Today Bestselling Author who prefers romantic fantasies to everyday reality. Fantasies take her to different times, races, places, and beyond. She lives with her husband, dog, several unnamed dust bunnies, and a black cat that can be scary or cuddly, depending on the current book. When she's not writing, Afton enjoys hiking, cooking, crafts, and reading.

Also by Afton Locke

Alpha in Disguise

Rebel's Claw